Anatomy of a Marine

Book 1
By
Gary L. Smiley

Edited by
Kathryn Anne Frey/Imagination Creative LLC
Front Image
Kathryn Anne Frey/Imagination Creative LLC

Table of Contents

Chapter One - Dazed and Confused

With the sun just over the horizon, our helicopter banked into a clearing and made a sloping decent toward the middle of an open field. Once the pilot gave us the "All Clear," the nine of us then jumped from the helicopter into shoulder high elephant grass and began running toward the safety of the jungle in front of us. Our helicopter climbed to a safe altitude, banked over the trees and immediately departed the area. With more than a hundred yards to negotiate, we weaved our way through the tall thick grass and uneven terrain, which seemed to slow us down with every step.

Then we began to receive automatic gunfire from the jungle in front of us. Before we knew what happened, three of my men were killed. The rest of us hit the ground scrambling for cover as enemy bullets ripped up the field around us. Once we were on the ground the enemy could not see us, but unfortunately, we could not see any of them, either.

The moment I hit the ground, I crawled until I reached a small knoll, which offered me some cover from the incoming bullets, but not much. With bullets striking all around me, I stayed low, raised my M-14 rifle and fired twenty rounds toward the jungle emptying my clip. That was my contribution in a somewhat futile attempt to suppress the enemy attack. With only six of us left, and limited resources, doing any real damage to the enemy would be nothing less than a miracle.

The enemy had positioned themselves securely along the tree line in front of us with excellent cover and a chance to pick us off one at a time. From the amount of muzzle flashes I saw before I hit the ground, we had to be out numbered at least four to one against machine guns, AK-47's, rocket-propelled grenades, and plenty of ammunition for the enemy to wage a small war against us.

As my men and I returned fire, I heard our radioman trying to make contact with the pilots to recall the chopper. I knew one thing for sure, without sufficient air cover from that helicopter our mission would be over before it started.

After I went through my second clip, I pulled my rifle back to reload, when an enemy bullet struck the stock of my rifle knocking it from my hands. The enemy soldiers were relentless in their efforts to take us all out before the helicopter returned. The enemy knew our helicopter would return, they were counting on it.

Even though we were pinned down with little cover, I still felt we had the advantage. All we had to do was stay alive until our helicopter arrived and suppressed the enemy long enough for us to slip into the jungle and out of sight. Unfortunately, we still had about a hundred yards to go before we reached the jungle, and our progress was going to be slow, even with the help of the chopper. That helicopter was our only salvation.

Then I heard a comforting sound. Our helicopter was arriving. When the helicopter came into view, the pilots positioned their craft to fire their rockets, as the gunner on board had already begun laying down a barrage of machine-gun fire into the tree line trying to suppress the enemy. The gunner was trying to hold the enemy off long enough for us to reach the safety of the jungle, but being pinned down with little cover, it was just too risky for me to order an advance.

Even with the helicopter, I felt it was best to sit tight and let the helicopter soften the enemy, or force them out of the area entirely. Once the helicopter had a chance to work its magic, and had the enemy scattering, I would then order my men to advance. But until then, it was best for the six of us to stay put. I knew I was making the right decision.

Then, in an instant, we lost control. As the chopper made its initial pass over us, I heard several enemy rounds clanking the side of our chopper, and the M-60 gunner on board was silenced. My heart dropped into my stomach, as I knew something was terribly wrong.

After the gunner was killed, the pilots swung around and fired their rockets into the tree line and then climbed to safety. When the rockets flew into the jungle and exploded, they missed their intended target doing little if any damage to the enemy. Without hesitation, the enemy continued to fire at us, as well as the chopper.

The moment our helicopter swung around for a second air strike, a barrage of enemy gunfire struck the craft, hitting the engine. When I looked behind me, I saw dark gray smoke spewing from the side of the helicopter. Our chopper was crippled and easy prey as it sputtered and smoked, trying to reach a safe altitude.

Before our helicopter had a chance to get out of the line of fire, an enemy rocket struck the tail section and knocked out the rear rotor. I watched in horror as the helicopter auto rotated into the ground and then exploded into pieces about fifty yards behind me. I then buried my face into the ground and covered my head as debris fell all around. There was nothing left of the helicopter but burning twisted wreckage and three dead crew members.

With their biggest obstacle destroyed, the enemy then turned their attention back to the six of us. In addition to a well-armed aggressive enemy who were determined to kill us all, unfortunately, we had a new problem. The fire from the burning chopper set the dry field on fire, which was moving toward us, cutting off any hope of a retreat. It was then I began to panic, for several reasons.

Since we had no air cover or an exit strategy and with a fire slowly approaching from behind, my men and I were left to fight it out with the enemy with less than a hundred rounds of ammunition each. We had no choice; it was either fight or die.

In our darkest moment I wanted to take charge, but I could not. I was already feeling the sting of defeat. My thoughts became erratic, and I began to second-guess myself instead of setting my fears aside and reacting as I was taught. But even though I was in a state of panic and confusion, an idea did occur to me. I needed to get to the radioman.

With very little courage left within me, I left my secure position and scurried through the grass toward the radioman. As I crawled, trying to make the smallest target possible, I could still hear my troops fighting it out with the enemy. The noise was deafening, blaring and so loud I could barely think.

In theory, I thought my idea was sound. My plan was to order a jet air strike, which would suppress the enemy long enough for my men and I to sneak into the jungle undetected. If the six of us could get into the jungle without getting killed, we would then have the element of surprise, and position ourselves behind the enemy, which could force them into the open reversing the situation. If all worked well, we could also have a chopper full of Marines flown in to corner the enemy soldiers in several different directions.

After crawling some fifty feet, I managed to spot my radioman. He was in the process of popping up and down, exchanging gunfire with the enemy and then quickly changing positions. Just as I got within a few feet of him, he stood to fire his rifle but caught a glimpse of me out of the corner of his eye. Because of that moment of hesitation a negative chain reaction took place, and all hell broke loose.

Within a split second of the radioman spotting me, a couple enemy rounds struck him in the chest knocking his feet completely from under him. His rifle twirled into the air, and he fell backwards landing on his side right in front of me. He was alive, but barely. He tried to open his mouth to say something, but the pain and confusion of the moment kept him from uttering a word.

After the radioman went down, I quickly crawled over and rolled him onto his back where I applied pressure and a bandage to his chest wounds. Frightened, I popped my head up trying to spot our medical corpsman. But no sooner did I lift my head than a bullet zinged dangerously close which forced me back to the ground.

In a state of panic, I turned my attention back to the wounded Marine. As I applied pressure to his injury, blood continued to run from his chest wounds, covering my hands. The harder I pushed on the bandage the guiltier I felt. I was responsible for the radioman getting shot. What was worse, I had no idea how to save him, or the rest of us for that matter. The radioman was about to die, and I knew it.

While I frantically worked to stop the bleeding, I was startled when the radioman grabbed at my uniform. He had a crazed look in his eyes, and I was not sure what he was trying to do. He took hold of my collar and began pulling me close as if he wanted to tell me something.

From what I could tell, he was trying to speak, but all I heard was the gurgling sound of fluid leaking into his lungs. He was drowning in his own blood and there was nothing I could do as I watched him struggle to gasp his last few breaths. The look in his eyes was horrible: the fear, the unknown, the helplessness, and then submission, knowing death was about to be his companion.

With all the energy he could muster, the radioman grabbed my hand, lifting it from his chest and placed it on the radio hand receiver lying next to my knee. He was not able to tell me verbally what he wanted, but I saw it in his eyes. He wanted me to radio for help before it was too late.

With the fire closing in and the enemy picking us off one at a time, he knew our situation was grim, and his last selfless act on this earth was to think of his fellow Marines. I didn't have the heart to tell him the radio had a bullet hole in it the size of a golf ball, and was useless. The bullets that passed through him also went straight through his radio rendering it useless.

Regardless, I reached for the handset. For the remaining moments he had left, I wanted him to think that we still had a chance to call for help.

As the radioman tightened his grip around my wrist, I felt the strength running from his body. Then, his grip on my arm grew weaker and weaker, and his hand relaxed, went limp and dropped. His body relaxed. His face went slack, and blood ran from his mouth. He was dead, but his eyes were still open, staring at me, which caused a shiver to run up and down my spine. I was so focused on the moment I had forgotten all about the gun battle taking place around me.

As I stared into the radioman's lifeless eyes, I then heard movement behind me. Reality suddenly set in and I was back in the game. As I spun around with my rifle at the ready, I just knew the enemy had managed to flank us from the rear. Fortunately, it was not the enemy; it was our medical corpsman running in my direction.

When the corpsman saw our radioman take a bullet, he made every effort to reach the wounded Marine to render aid. While lying on my back out of the way of the bullets, I motioned for the corpsman to hit the deck, but it was too late. With only a few feet to go before reaching me, a bullet struck the corpsman in the back of his right leg, knocking him to his knees. I saw a hole rip open the front of his thigh and bone and flesh flew into the air. When the corpsman hit his knees, I saw him clutch his thigh in pain and drop his pistol and medical kit. The look on his face was horrible.

The second the corpsman hit the ground; I quickly sat up and lunged forward in an attempt to pull him out of the line of fire. Unfortunately, I was not fast enough. The moment I reached up for his arm, several bullets passed through the corpsman's upper body, blowing pieces of his flesh and blood onto my face and chest. I let go of the corpsman and rolled away, thinking the next bullet had to be meant for me.

It all happened so fast, it felt as if everything were moving in slow motion. Then I was jolted back to reality when the body of the corpsman fell on me, dead before he hit the ground. The second the body flopped on top of me, I could feel the warm blood running from his body, soaking my uniform. When that happened, 1 panicked and had to get from underneath the corpsman and as far away from him as possible. With all the energy I could muster, I sat up only long enough to roll the body aside.

The heavy weight of the corpsman's body rolled limp onto the ground, where dirt stuck to the smeared blood that covered his face. Then I paused when I thought for sure I heard him say something. But that was impossible, because he was dead, and I knew that my mind had to be playing tricks on me.

As I sat up and stared into his lifeless eyes, another bullet zinged dangerously close to my head, nearly making me the sixth victim. Once again I dove for the safety of the ground using the body of my two dead friends for cover as I tried to think of another plan to get the rest of us out alive.

I couldn't believe what was happening. We were supposed to have the advantage and the element of surprise, but we didn't. We were being chopped to shreds and there was nothing we could do to prevent it. When I realized that, on the average, I was losing a man a minute, I then knew the situation was beyond my control. As I sat there in a state of panic, I wanted to quit, and turn the controls over to someone more qualified.

But there was no one to lead the team but me, and based on that thought, I knew I had to do something fast, or the rest of us would soon meet the same fate as our friends. With five of my men dead, and a blanket of smoke covering the field, each of us were growing weaker by the moment and our ammunition was extremely low. I had lost all confidence in my ability to see the mission through, but it was either take action or die.

The enemy had us cornered and they knew it. It was just a matter of time before the enemy gained the confidence to come out of the jungle, or the fire pushed us toward them. I was running out of options and the thought of getting out alive began to slip farther and farther from my survival mentality. Regardless, I had to try something before it was too late.

With the barrage of enemy gunfire continuing to rip past me, I got to my feet determined to reach my men and take them to safety. But no sooner was I on my feet when a bullet ricocheted off the side of my helmet, knocking it from my head. It all happened so fast; I did not remember hitting the ground. While trying to pull myself together, I rolled onto my back and inserted a new ammo clip into my rifle, but it was difficult with my hands shaking.

I was so scared. As I lay on the ground I tried to get back in the fight, but every nerve in my body became numb and my courage was nonexistent. With a thousand thoughts flying in and out of my head, I knew there had to be a way to survive. I was not about to give up, but it was hard to keep my head when my men were dying all around me.

With my ears still ringing from my near death experience, I found the courage to once again get up and join my men. Just as I decided to get back in the fight, I heard another one of my men take a bullet as he tried to advance on the enemy. He, too, was dead. At least my men had the courage to fight. All I could do was run and hide while my men suffered the consequences. With six of my men dead, there were only three of us left to fight it out against thirty or more enemy soldiers.

Once I got to my feet, I began firing my rifle trying to reach my two remaining men who were some forty yards ahead of me. I spotted them both up ahead of me, and three steps later a searing pain struck me in the right shoulder, spinning me like a top. At first I saw the jungle, then the burning helicopter and finally, the sky. The impact of the bullet spun me around and knocked me to the ground where I lost my sense of direction, not to mention my rifle, which was out of reach.

With a throbbing and burning pain shooting through my bleeding shoulder, I tried to locate my backpack to get my medical kit, but I somehow lost it in the fall. Actually, I was so scared I wasn't even sure I had a medical kit. Regardless, with no medical kit or morphine to ease the pain, I applied pressure to my wound, but any movement caused excruciating pain to shoot through my shoulder, arm and back.

The pain made me dizzy as I began to drift in and out of consciousness. While lying in a puddle of my own blood nursing my shoulder wound, I could hear my two remaining troops fighting it out with the enemy. Their ammunition had to be nearly gone, but I knew they were not about to give up the fight as they made every attempt to work their way toward the jungle.

With labored breathing and no feeling in my right arm, I crawled around on my back trying to locate the corpsman's medical kit. I needed a vial of morphine, but it too was nowhere in sight.

With my left arm I continued to apply pressure to my bleeding shoulder, but I was losing a lot of blood and needed help. My wound was too severe to handle alone. But I knew the score. No one was coming to help me, only kill me.

With thick smoke blanketing the area, it became difficult for me to see. I then began to cough, which was the worst thing to do because it gave away my position. I was scared beyond belief. The end was near. I could feel it deep in my soul. With most of my men killed, a bullet in my shoulder, and a fire pushing us closer to the enemy, I was willing to give up the fight. For some reason the thought of death gave me comfort.

While listening to my two remaining troops exchange fire with the enemy, something happened. All the shooting stopped. I gritted my teeth, and closed my eyes, listening. The enemy was on the move. They had left the jungle and were moving in our direction. I could hear them running toward us. They were coming to finish us off. We were about to die, and there was nothing any of us could do to prevent it.

With nothing to lose, my two remaining troops got to their feet firing their weapons while charging toward the enemy. My men were not about to be tortured or spend what was left of their lives in a POW camp. They knew they were about to die, and with what little bullets they had left, they would take as many of the enemy with them as possible. At least they had the courage to fight.

Once again the enemy opened fire. I heard the bullets hit my men, and then their bodies hit the ground. The enemy bullets slowed, and then stopped. Faintly, I could smell gunpowder. It was quiet but I knew the enemy had to be moving in my direction. The only sounds I heard were the crackling of the burning chopper behind me. With all of my troops dead, the only thing I could think of was my own survival.

I wanted to devise a plan to escape, but I was not sure how to make that happen. I was too weak to run, and not lucid enough to fight. The pain in my shoulder was getting worse. I could not stop the bleeding and I had no sensation in my fingers. With clouded thoughts, the only thing I could do was pretend to be dead when the enemy walked upon me. Then, I heard them. They were closing in on me.

The sounds of the enemy footsteps were getting closer. They were only a few yards away, and all around me. They made no effort to conceal their location as their heavy steps brushed through the tall grass. I closed my eyes pretending to be dead. I held my breath. I tried to think of a prayer, but my mind went blank.

Suddenly, a few more rounds were fired by the enemy, but not at me. They fired a short burst, maybe five or six rounds. They must have found one of my men alive. When I heard the shot, I flinched. Thankfully, they were not close enough to see me twitch. After they had finished off one of my troops the soldiers were on the move again, and they were moving in my direction.

The enemy had fanned out through the field approaching from different directions, getting closer and closer. They were so close I was sure they could see me sprawled out in the tall grass. I kept thinking to myself, "If they discovered that I was alive, would they kill me, torture me, or just take me as a prisoner of war?" At the time it really didn't matter. Regardless, there was a good possibility that I would bleed out or burn to death before they reached me.

Then, two enemy soldiers walked upon me and stopped. They were so close I could smell them. I held my breath, and my eyes were closed. They were standing at the base of my feet, talking. I could not understand their words. I smelled a burning cigarette. I remained perfectly still hoping one of them would not empty his clip into me.

With my eyes closed I could visualize them cautiously moving around, crouched over with their rifles pointing at me looking for the slightest movement, ready to fire a few short bursts into me. I did not open my eyes, or breathe for that matter. I only prayed the smoke did not make me cough.

Suddenly, one of the soldiers put an ammo clip in his rifle, jerked the bolt back and released it. It frightened me, but I remained motionless. I had a mental image of a rifle pointed at my head and a finger squeezing the trigger. The soldiers must have known that I was still alive, otherwise, why were they hovering over me? Why had they not searched me for maps or shot me, for that matter, just to be sure? I just knew that a bullet would soon pierce my body ending all my worries.

But I was wrong. The ambushers were on the move again. As a few others walked toward me, I could feel their eyes, and hear their steps only inches from my head. Their footsteps were so close. From the sounds, there appeared to be seven or eight of them on both sides of me. At some distance, I could hear several others walking through the grass, talking, and searching the area.

As the enemy moved away from me their sounds began to fade. The soldiers were moving toward the burning chopper. They wanted to admire their kill. That downed chopper might have been my only salvation. As long as the soldiers were moving away, it would give me a chance to slip into the jungle undetected before they discovered I was missing.

My plan was to get into the jungle and hide. The way I figured it, a search party would eventually come looking, and I would be rescued. But even if I made it safely into the jungle, how long could I survive while bleeding profusely, with no access to food or water? Besides, I was not even sure what direction I was pointing. Behind me I heard a couple of the enemy soldiers laugh as they moved toward the remains of the downed helicopter.

As the enemy moved farther away their sounds began to fade. I had to take the risk and try to escape. With what little energy I had left, I slowly lifted my eyelids but it was difficult due to the dried blood that covered my eyes. Besides, the thought of what I might see was as painful as the bullet in my shoulder. I didn't know what to expect.

What if there was one or more of them standing over me with a rifle pointed at my head. What would I do? Worse yet, what would the enemy soldier do? But I had to take the chance. I did not know how long it would be before the soldiers came back for me. I struggled, but I finally managed to get my eyes open.

As the first ray of light entered, I saw only swaying grass before me, and the arm of one of my troops covered in blood. Slowly, I turned my head looking in all directions, but saw no one. Thank the Lord.

To get a better look around, I rose onto my left elbow, but the effort caused excruciating pain to shoot through my shoulder. It was so bad, I nearly passed out. The pain in my shoulder hurt so bad, it took everything I had to keep from screaming at the top of my lungs. I knew that one wrong utterance of pain, or ruffle of the grass could very well cost me my life. I tried to remain quiet, but it was difficult with the threat of death lurking in every direction.

Once I was up on my elbow, every vein in my neck and forehead had to be bulging, about to explode from the pain I was experiencing. My body was so cold and I began to shake all over. Then, out of nowhere, a euphoric feeling came over me that all was well. At that particular moment anything could have happened to me and I would not have cared.

Then, as I scanned the area in front of me, I saw the body of one of my troops lying off to my right side. His body was riddled with bullets and blood covered nearly his entire uniform. The fact that I was still alive and the rest of my men were dead made me sick to my stomach. When I saw the dead body and all the blood, a sudden rush of guilt ran through my body and I thought to myself, "This was my first mission as a Sergeant leading troops and I let my men…"

Just as I tried to scurry through the grass toward the jungle, suddenly, an enemy soldier rose from a kneeling position beyond the grass in front of me. He advanced toward me, crouched over with his rifle pointing toward me, but for some reason he had not fired.

As the soldier approached, my eyes were fixed firmly on the barrel of the rifle aimed directly at my chest. I had no way to defend myself. With my rifle not in reach, all I had for protection was my K-Bar knife, which I had planned to use as a tool to help me crawl toward the jungle. When the enemy inched closer with his finger firmly on the trigger, I froze, thinking that any second a blast to the chest would end all my worrying, forever.

I opened my mouth to speak, but no words came out. Then, I saw a bright flash. Again, a sharp pain pierced my right shoulder. The soldier shot me in nearly the same spot. The impact threw me against the ground with a thundering force. I was rolling left and right, the pain was horrifying. The blood, which ran from my body, was warm, and in a way comforting, euphoric.

When I discovered that I was still alive, and with nothing to lose, I once again opened my eyes. I needed to see the face of the person trying to kill me. With limited vision, I saw the silhouette of my enemy, or should I say, my killer. The sun was fixed perfectly behind the head of my assassin, making it too bright for me to make out the contours of his face.

As the sun obscured most of my vision, I could partially see the soldier's head and something that covered it, which I thought looked something like a baby's blanket. But as my vision came into focus, allowing me a better look at the face, I saw that my attacker was not a man, but instead, a young girl about fifteen years old. In one hand she had an AK-47 and in the other she was cradling a small child, doing her best to balance them both.

Upon a second glance I noticed the baby was not moving.

In fact, the child was limp in her arms. I was sure the child had been killed. The baby was possibly killed from the array of bullets we poured into the tree line. As I stared at its lifeless body it was almost hard to believe. For the briefest moment I felt no pain in my shoulder or concern for my situation. I actually felt some compassion for the girl's loss. Besides, what the hell was a baby doing in the middle of a jungle battle?

Back in America, a girl her age would be at a slumber party gossiping about her boyfriend and swapping rock & roll records. But that would never happen in this country. The young girl, if she lives another day, will be lucky to have rat meat or dung beetles for her next meal. Her situation was definitely grim and she had not an ounce of compassion for her enemy...me.

The girl stood motionless, staring at me as if she had never seen a human before. Her face was tense and her lips were pulled tight over her teeth. Her eyes were locked on mine and sported the look of hate, disgust, and anger within them. One wrong move from me and I knew that I was a dead man.

The weapon she struggled to hold was pointed directly at my chest. From the look on her face, there was no way I was about to leave the field alive. But why had she not killed me? Only seconds had passed since she shot me, but why had she not finished me off, or her comrades not ran back to her? Was she enjoying the moment by watching me bleed out, or was she having second thoughts about what she had done? Either way, my life was about to be over. At that very moment, my confidence level was below par and dropping rapidly.

Thinking as fast as my distorted thoughts would allow, I reached out to her as if to ask for help while nursing the two bullet holes in my shoulder. I tried to slowly crawl to her, but every inch I moved in her direction forced her to take a step back, gripping her weapon all the tighter.

With the amount of blood I had lost, I made one last effort to appeal to her compassionate side, if there were such a thing. I somehow thought that she might set her weapon on the ground and attend to my wounds. But she was not a nun, nor a medic. She was the enemy.

I motioned for her to come closer and help me. I pulled my hand off of my right shoulder to expose my wound, which had a steady stream of blood dripping from it. For a moment, I thought she might take pity on me.

My plan was not working. I noticed her finger quivering, as it lay across the trigger of her weapon, ready to use it if necessary. But what was keeping her from killing me? If this situation were reversed, I wouldn't be standing there hesitating. I would have finished her off and not given it a second thought.

Oh, yes, given the chance, I would kill her. We were not in America, and little Miss AK-47 was not a prom queen. If I managed to get close enough, she would be dead in a matter of seconds.

With the other members of her team moving farther away, it was time for me to make my move. It might be my only opportunity to escape. I was on my own and for me, time was running out, and I was hallucinating. I thought I could hear music. I knew the truth. There would be no last minute miracle rescue. There would be no cavalry charging over the hill with guns a blazing. There would be no last minute helicopter full of Marines dropping from the sky to scoop me from the clutches of death. I had to escape. I had to get past my last obstacle.

The only thing that stood between me and the safety of the jungle was the scared little girl in front of me. It was either kill her or to have my corpse rot away in an open field for the animals to feast on. At that moment I had the advantage, even in my condition. She was a kid, for God's sake. I could take her because she had not seen the knife I had hidden under my arm. I was confident that my knife would soon pierce her lung, not allowing her to yell out for help, and then I would move on to plan B.

The young girl then began blinking as if coming out of a trance. As I looked into her eyes, it made me think that I somehow knew her. I set those thoughts aside and decided to make my move. I then lunged at her with my knife. The stalemate was over. The moment I made my move the girl fired off three rounds, with only one of her bullets striking me in my right shoulder, knocking me back to the ground. A tearing pain ripped through my shoulder, and blood ran down my arm, soaking my sleeve. Determined to fight to the last, I sat straight up, stabbing at my killer as my last act of defiance. I would not die like a coward.

The moment my eyes were open I was startled to see my daughter standing beside my bed, poking me in the shoulder with the handle of a golf club. She was wide-eyed and shocked. She was prepared to run, not knowing what her dad might do next.

As she stood there with my golf club in one hand and a stuffed animal in the other, in a slow, frightened voice, she said, "Dad, are you all right? Come on Dad, wake up. You were dreaming."

Confused, I looked around the room and said, "What happened? Where am I?"

She reluctantly replied, "Dad, you had a nightmare. You

were thrashing around so much I thought you were having a seizure or something. You scared the crap out of me. You must have been dead to the world, because I could hear you moaning all the way down stairs. Who were you yelling at?"

My daughter then dropped the golf club, put her hands on her hips and said in a quivering voice, "Dad, why are you having so many nightmares? You're scaring me. Can't your doctors give you something for that?"

While I lay there breathing hard and trying to focus my eyes, I replied, "It's no big deal, sweetie, the nightmares are the least of my problems. They're just something I need to work through. You don't have to worry. I'll be fine."

She then wiped up her eyes, picked up the golf club, and said, "Well, you better get a move on. It's time for you to get up. Besides, didn't you say something about an important meeting at the Veterans Administration this morning? You better get going or you're going to be late."

As I sat up staring at my daughter, my head was spinning, my heart pounding. I was drenched in sweat, and my alarm clock was blaring with the sounds of a local radio station. I tried to focus, to get an understanding of my surroundings. Then it occurred to me. My troops were not dead, nor was I. While wiping the sweat from my eyes, I glanced up and watched as my daughter placed the golf club back in the bag, and slowly began to walk from my bedroom.

Somewhat conscious and relieved that I was not dead, I propped up on both elbows trying to focus my vision and I said in a shaky voice, "Thanks, Dad's up… now." My daughter waved, but didn't turn around.

When she left the room, I fell back onto my pillow and sighed with relief. My entire body was quivering, and for some reason my right shoulder hurt. I then looked at my shoulder just to make sure I didn't have any bullet holes. Of course I wasn't shot, but I could not figure out why my shoulder ached.

Slowly, I rolled out of bed and got to my feet using the wall for support. I was so weak and scared that my legs were shaking, which caused them to buckle, nearly throwing me into the wall. As I leaned against the wall for support, my mind began to clear. It was all coming back to me.

With a hundred thoughts a second running through my head, I paused ever so briefly to catch my breath and wipe the sweat from my forehead again. Breathing rapidly, my hands shaking and sweating profusely, I felt like I just returned from a marathon run.

When I leaned over with my hands on my knees, I began to laugh, thankful that it was only a dream. Then a sense of calm came over me. I was so relieved that it was only a dream. But it wasn't a dream. It was a fucking nightmare. My nightmare was so clear and real that I actually believed I was experiencing the death of my men, the pain and the bleeding from my wounds. I had never experienced anything so real.

Glancing over at my bed, I saw my pillow and sheets were soaked with sweat, but I wasn't surprised. I had gone through shit like this before, on several occasions. But lately, the dreams seemed to be getting worse. Most nights I dread going to sleep for fear of what lurks deep within my mind, or worse, what might surface because of it. Someone once said that sleep for some is a blessing, but for others, it's a nightmare. They weren't bullshitting.

Grateful to be alive, and wanting to sit and reflect on my nightmare, I noticed the time. I had about ten minutes before I had to leave for the Boulder Vet Center. It was five after eight, and I had to be in Boulder by nine. Unfortunately, I had a forty-five minute drive to look forward to, and in winter weather.

Stumbling into the shower, my mind was focused on nothing but the hell I just lived through. After taking a quick five-minute shower, I bolted downstairs, buttoning my shirt, and running my hands through my hair to somewhat comb it.

I went through the kitchen, picking up my keys and cell phone, trying not to focus on the three hours of sleep I just received, which was a lot considering my sleep habits. Groggy, I felt like I was walking around in a fog as everything was closing in around me.

After grabbing the essential equipment, I walked through the kitchen toward the back door, heading for the garage.

"Dad!" The sound of my daughter's voice startled me. I quickly turned to see her leaning against the counter with her hand extended. She said, "Dad, you forgot this." She handed me a cup of coffee and then patted me on the back. "You better get going, mister, or you are going to be late."

I smiled at her and said, "Thanks, sweetie, I have to get going." I then turned toward the back door.

My daughter, Casi, was only six when my wife and I divorced ten years ago, and through luck, I managed to get custody of her, or should I say, she got custody of me. As anyone who knows me can tell you, living with me is not an easy thing to do. It's been even harder for a sixteen-year-old girl with a nut for a father. Casi has grown up fast. I tell people that she is sixteen going on thirty and she earned every minute of it.

But she is a good daughter and knows what is wrong with me. Over the past few years, she's seen me go through several nightmares, anxiety attacks and damn near a mental breakdown, but regardless, she stayed with me through the thick of it all. She knows when to step in and step out of my life. My mind was clearing, but something occurred to me.

As I was unlocking the back door I stopped, turned and said, "Hey, aren't you supposed to be in school today?"

She turned, grinned and rolled her eyes replying, "Dad, it's Christmas break!"

Standing there with a somewhat stupid look on my face, I turned to her with my blood shot eyes and mumbled in a confused voice, "It's Christmas break, you're kidding me? Okay, that's right, I remember now." That was bullshit. I didn't remember, but I knew my daughter was not about to lie to me.

Casi laughed, rolled her eyes and walked into the family room waving goodbye to me without looking back.

I made it to my jeep before I realized that it was the month of December. Over the past few months, I'd been mentally detached due to the past surfacing into the present, affecting the direction of my future. I drove away thinking about my very real nightmare, and what the rest of this day holds for me, not to mention my future.

Chapter Two - The Drifter

Weaving my jeep in and out of city traffic and trying to negotiate the icy roads, I was rushing to my meeting at the Veteran's Center in Boulder, Colorado, and I was about to be late. This wasn't my first time at the center, and it certainly wouldn't be my last. I was a regular there twice a week: On Monday, I attended group therapy with other veterans where we discussed the stress in our lives and how it affected us on daily basis. Then on Thursday, I attend a one-on-one session with my psychologist, Doctor Easton, whom I'd been seeing for the past few weeks. We had scheduled two sessions but I'd only attended one. I was a busy man.

But today was different. It was Friday and Dr. Easton asked me to attend a special session at the V.A. to discuss a series of problems I was having at my place of work. It's entirely my fault. Because of bad judgment in trusting the management staff with sensitive information on my PTSD, the company accused me of being a threat to the workplace. Since they considered me a danger, they sent me home for an unspecified amount of time, without pay, until they determined what to do with me. They wanted me fired, and the sooner I was gone, the better.

The worst part of this nightmare scenario was that I'd be losing an eighty thousand-dollar a year job, plus benefits. If that happened, it would put my financial situation into a proverbial tailspin, and I couldn't let that happen. For me, that would create a negative chain of events, which could spiral me right into a dark abyss and homelessness and in the process, I could lose custody of my daughter. There was no way I could have that shit. Dr. Easton wasn't about to let me get fired, not if he could help it. He had talked to human resources at my place of work and vowed to get to the bottom of the problem. They agreed to hold off, temporarily. I pulled my jeep in and parked.

I entered the main double doors and stomped the snow off my boots. I walked through the waiting room, which was usually full of people, but for some reason, it was empty. I stopped and poured myself a cup of coffee, then looking at my watch I walked down the corridor with seconds to spare.

At the end of the hall I heard the conference room door open and saw Doctor Easton walking toward me with a concerned look. I stepped aside as he passed me saying, "Hey, buddy, how you doing? Go in the conference room and make yourself comfortable. We have another situation brewing, and I just need a few minutes to deal with this before you and I get started." I gave the doctor a gracious nod, stepped into the room, took a seat, and used my coffee cup as a hand warmer. Then I began to think.

After about five minutes of waiting, I became bored. And when I'm bored, I have trouble sitting still. And when I can't sit still, I need something to keep me busy. So, instead of sitting there thinking about the barrage of questions Doctor Easton would be asking; I began to kill time by focusing on the various objects around the room to occupy my mind and avoid dying of boredom.

As I looked around, I noticed the walls to the left were covered with action pictures of U.S. combat troops in Vietnam, while the back wall had the American Flag patriotically displayed above a desk. The desk was cluttered with a computer under repair, a printer, and a ton of papers in disarray, like someone had been searching for something. The walls on the right had shelves of books about America's last three big wars, and several videotapes of Hollywood war movies such as The Green Berets, Full Metal Jacket, The Sands of Iwo Jima, the Hunt for Red October, and so on.

Then something caught my attention. I began to focus on a two-foot long model helicopter hanging from the ceiling, slowly spinning in circles from a light breeze from an open-air vent. After a couple minutes of focusing on the helicopter, I began to hear faint distant noises like screams, crashing, and pleas for help. My thoughts began to drift in and out, and the noises outside began to fade as if someone had turned the volume down. Then, before I knew it, all the noises were gone, and so was I, mentally.

(The medical corpsman and I work our way through the jungle to the edge of the crash site and I pause to catch my breath. The jungle's so hot that I can barely breathe. The heat's over a hundred degrees and the humidity's a hundred percent and sweat drips steadily from my face onto my camouflage uniform.

Needing a break, I lean against a tree and begin nursing my back wound as every movement sends a sharp pain radiating down my lower back and legs, making it difficult for me to move around. From head to foot I'm aching, cut, scraped, bleeding, and any walking or strain of any kind causes a grinding in my lower back. I'm beginning to think my back might be broken. Even though I'm in pain, I'm still on my feet, and determined to help my troops.

As I move around the tree with my pistol firmly in hand, I maneuver for a better look at the destruction that lay before me. But my vision was obscured by the pollution of thick black smoke that covers the crash site like that of an early morning fog. As I step from behind the tree I have my first glimpse of the horrors that befell my comrades. Everything seems to be moving in slow motion as my eyes are fixed upon the dead, the wounded, and the remains of what was once a CH-53 transport helicopter.

When I look toward the top of the hill where the chopper started its deadly decent, I see a three hundred foot gaping path down the hillside where the chopper's last moments moved aside trees, rocks, and foliage, gouging out large portions of the earth. In its wake it left behind hundreds of pieces of fiberglass, rotors, and bodies, as it had rolled to the bottom of the hill, burning what was left of its crippled remains.

As I look upon the dead and wounded that were sprawled from the top of the hill down to the belly of the beast, I counted eighteen bodies that I could see, but I knew there were more, plenty more. Whether they're dead or not, I have no idea. Then I spot number nineteen. Close to the top of the hill, one of the crew chiefs from the helicopter hung by his neck in the forks of a tree. His body swayed in the breeze from the hovering helicopters above and he was visible to all, like that of a public hanging right out of the old west.

A medical corpsman ran past me yelling, "Jesus, Sergeant, let's go, there are wounded over there!" My breathing's shallow and rapid as I use my forearm to wipe the sweat from my eyes to clear my vision. With all the energy I can muster, and with pain radiating down my back and legs, I push myself from the tree and struggle toward the heart of the crash, and all the dead.

A few steps into my trek something got caught between the toe of my rear foot and the heel of my front foot, causing me to fall flat on my face. From the pain it felt as if someone had driven a stake through my lower back. Lying there, I spread my hands into a push-up position to raise my upper body enough to slowly roll over onto my back. I land with such a jolt, I yell out in pain.

In anger, and with all the energy I can muster, I use my elbows to raise myself to see the object that caused my fall. There before me I see what's left of a human arm, lying on a branch at the base of my feet. The arm had been sheered off below the elbow, and the hand was laying in such a way that the index finger was pointing at me with the other fingers and thumb formed into a semi-fist. It sends a cold chill up and down my spine.

I release and fall onto my back, resting for a moment. Then, using my elbows I roll over on my stomach, get to my knees, pick up the arm, and hold it loosely in my hands. To relieve some of the tension on my aching back, I lean into a somewhat sitting position and begin to examine the detached appendage. Why I doing this I have no idea.

The arm had turned a gray color and was cold to the touch. From where the arm was cut I could see the muscle and the bones, but something strange catches my attention. There's no blood. Then something else occurs to me. Where was the rest of this Marine's body? Moving slowly, I look around the immediate area but spot nothing but helicopter debris and military equipment.

Because of the smoke that engulfs the entire area I began to cough, which again causes sharp pains reminding me of what needs attention. There's something else. There's a smell in the air I can't recognize, which smells like beer poured over hot charcoal coals. The smell is disgusting, and I later discover that it was burning flesh.

Slowly setting the arm on the ground in front of me, I place my hands on my thighs and push my upper body vertical, leaning back onto my boots as every inch of movement causes the radiating pain in my back to increase.

Faintly, I hear my name being called. To my right and just inside the thicket of the jungle I spot a friend of mine lying on his back reaching toward me. It's Sergeant Crow. He's mumbling something, but I can't hear him. He's been seriously wounded from the helicopter crash and is holding a helmet tight against his stomach with blood seeping from beneath it. My friend wants to tell me something but I'm unable to make out what he was saying. I need to get to him. I'm not about to let him die like this. Making every effort to get to my feet I work to push myself vertical when I hear a voice say, "Gary, are you with me?" Tired and in pain, I raise my head to respond.)

Chapter Three - Back In Boulder

Looking up I see Dr. Easton, his lips were moving but I heard very little. He was asking if I was okay but my mind was still someplace else. Then it occurred to me. I wasn't at the crash site. I was sitting in my doctor's office with his eyes fixed firmly upon me. Then I saw him sit down and take a sip of coffee, then set it on the table next to him. It looked as if he were moving in slow motion. My mind began to clear and my surroundings began to focus, including that fucking model helicopter spinning above my head. Reality suddenly set in, or at least that's what I thought. Hell, for all I knew I could have still been at the crash site or in another dimension.

Reluctantly I raised my head, exhaled heavily and wondered what Dr. Easton must have thought of me at that moment. Not only was I zoning in and out, my hair was a mess, I needed a shave, my clothes were worn and wrinkled, and my eyes were blood shot from three hours of sleep the night before. I looked more like a homeless man than a veteran seeking help for PTSD. Trying to come out of my mental fog, which clouded my vision, I knew I somehow needed to recover from my embarrassing sideshow without looking like I needed a long stay in the rubber room.

Speaking before I had a chance to think, which I am definitely good at, I replied, "Yeah, I'm fine, doc, I haven't been sleeping well lately; I just dozed off, sorry." Still looking directly at me, Doctor Easton slightly nodded. He knew my comments were bullshit, and I could tell he was curious about what he'd just seen, and why I needed to lie about it.

Dr. Easton leaned back, crossed his legs, and in a quiet voice asked, "Gary, were you dozing off, meditating, or just in deep thought?" He never brought up the idea that I might be having a flashback, and I was glad he didn't.

Sitting with my arms crossed, I began tapping my foot, embarrassed from my mental sideshow. I was hoping he'd just let it go. I wanted to answer but didn't know the right words. Looking up and in a low voice, I answered, "Well, sometimes I tend to drift in and out, especially when I'm confronted with situations, like today! Old memories surface to remind me of the past, and I'm constantly reminded that I'm not allowed to forget the past- whatever the fuck that means. But it's nothing, doc, really, I'm okay now." I then clapped my hands together and said, "If you don't mind I'd like to get this over with so I can go home. All of a sudden I don't feel so good, and could use some time alone."

Dr. Easton looked concerned as he sat up and leaned onto the armrest. He started to say something, but paused. There was a moment of uncomfortable silence and then he calmly said, "You sure you are okay? Because if you need some time we can take a break to give you a chance to pull yourself together. You want to take five and have a smoke? I'll go outside with you if you want!" He then leaned forward with coffee cup in hand as if ready to get up and escort me outside for a cigarette. Dr. Easton's a good guy. You know what I mean...a vet knows a vet.

Feeling that I wasn't about to be questioned into the void about my mental drift, I answered with more enthusiasm, "Nah, really, I'm fine. I just happened to get a little side tracked is all and the stress tends to take the strength out of me. I'll be all right as we move along here. I think it's okay if we get started."

This is only my second session with Dr. Easton, but the first time we met, it's like we'd known each other for years.

When we first talked, Dr. Easton listened to my many problems and how the weight of the world burdens my life. He is a pleasant looking man, around five feet ten inches, easy going if you will, and a true professional in every way. He's in his mid-fifties with sandy blonde hair that has a touch of gray along his sideburns. Whenever he speaks, it's always in a quiet, peaceful voice, and even though he had years of experience dealing with veterans, he tells me that I'm his most challenging case. Doctor Easton cares about his patients and he would never let anyone take advantage of a Veteran. Dr. Easton's a good friend, and no matter how the day or my career turned out, I know there's at least one person in my corner helping me throw punches.

Dr. Easton said, "Well, let's see if we can find a starting point here. To begin with, I received a call about your problems at work. I'm sure they're no different than the previous ones you've been having with your co-workers. And from the call, it seems your job is hanging by a thread, if you haven't already been fired. So if you don't mind, what I would like to do today is ask some questions on a variety of subjects. I want to start with your family, where you grew up, and your family members as well. Then, I'd like to hear about the PTSD and how it's shifted into high gear over the last few weeks. I also want you to bring me up to speed on your problems at work and how you managed to get yourself in such a serious situation that's about to get you fired."

"Finally, if you are up to it, let's try to get to your military missions overseas, especially since we've never touched on any of your military experiences. Now some of this might be hard to talk about, but do the best you can, and if at any time you feel that you may need a break, just speak up and we'll stop. Do you have any questions so far?"

Doctor Easton then reached for his coffee, slowly putting it up to his mouth.

I shifted in my seat and said. "Well, doc, I'm ready when you are. Let's get this over with so I can go back to see what creative ways human resources have come up with to fire me today."

Dr. Easton looked at me and said, "Let's start slow with some mental calisthenics before we get into the heavy dialogue. I'd like for you to begin by telling me a little about your family, where you grew up, any siblings you might have, and how you came to join the Marines. I'm not looking for any details here, just give me the broad strokes. We'll get more into the details when we address to your problems at work and military missions. So, whenever you're ready. Take as much time as you need. Remember, we're not on the clock here."

I thought for a second and wondered just how far down the rabbit hole I wanted to take Doctor Easton. My family experience was something unique and I wasn't sure that telling the whole story would be needed, but it might be necessary. Then I decided to start at the beginning and just let story unfold.

Chapter Four - The Contrarian

As a child I grew up in Tennessee, the youngest of four children. My dad was Grady and my mom was Annie. They'd been married for some eighteen years and were in their mid forties when I arrived as their last little bundle of joy. My sister, Scarlett, was my next oldest sibling and ten years my senior, and was in constant battles with my two older brothers who harassed her on a daily basis. My brothers were Rhett and Brent, who were named, along with my sister, after movie characters from "Gone with the Wind." My brothers were fourteen and sixteen years old when I entered this privileged life, and they picked on me every chance they got.

From the day I was born, I was spoiled, babied, shadowed by helpers, had everything handed to me, including money, and I knew life no other way. Unfortunately, my brothers and sister were not so lucky. They grew up in a time when our family had very little and had to struggle for money, for food, for decent clothing and were ridiculed by classmates for wearing worn out hand-me-down clothes. And of course, my brothers struggled on the farm during the harvest season helping to bring in the crops, which paid our family very little, if anything, in the way of money. Our family was always broke, and a lot of the time, hungry.

Then, our lives changed. In a shrewd business deal, our father sold off some 2000 worthless acres of our land to some desperate developers looking to build a country club on the outskirts of our small town. No one could believe it. An investment company wanted to develop a large parcel of land for a country club and golf course that would intersect with three other farms in the area.

It was a great opportunity for our family. And my father, being a good horse trader, not only sold our property for $400 an acre, but he managed to negotiate 1% of the country club profits due to our land being crucial to the developer's deal.

After it was all said and done, in 1950 our family was no longer poor. We had over $885,000 dollars from the sale of our property and a percentage of the country club profits. The interesting thing here was that the country club was a hit. No one ever thought it would get off the ground, much less be a success.

Out of our sleepy farming community of 25,000 people, 75% were poor, but 25% of the population had money to burn. And the ones with money, they wanted to live like movie stars, act special, and look rich, so they showed up in droves to join the new club.

Dad was a genius. Besides selling off our land, he invested in anything that would sell to the members of the country club. He knew those people had a pocket full of money and he was about to capitalize on it. After a little planning, my father built a hotel about a mile from the country club where all the phony members had their relatives stay when visiting. The hotel was booked year round and so successful, Dad even thought about building a second hotel to accommodate the extra business.

He then made other small business investments around the country club: a couple of full service gas stations, a souvenir store, a department store, a liquor store with a drive up window, and finally, a fast food eatery (as they called them back then), so members from the country club could grab a quick bite as they headed for home or wherever. Every business Dad opened was a success.

This all worked out well for our family, especially me, since

I was born two years after we were considered millionaires. We were rolling in the money. People used to hate us for being poor and sometimes wouldn't sell to us in town, but once the money started rolling in, the townspeople couldn't kiss our family's ass fast enough. After making all that money, our family then had respect, plenty of food, new clothes, cars, and college educations. So needless to say, I grew up a lot different than my brothers and sister.

Since Mom was so busy helping Dad with the business, they decided to hire some help to look after me. When I was two, my parents hired a black nanny named Ms. Birdie, and everyone in the family respected her. Ms. Birdie didn't have much after her husband was killed in the Korean War, and after a couple years, Ms. Birdie and her son, Jeremiah, came to live with us. Dad had remodeled a storage facility we had on the property and turned it into a nice place to live, all furnished and with electricity and running water. Ms. Birdie loved it there, especially when Dad told her she didn't have to pay any rent.

Ms. Birdie took good care of me. I was known as her brown-eyed baby doll, but she referred to my rowdy brothers and sister as, "You little white shits." When Ms. Birdie went to town for supplies, she took her son Jeremiah and me right along with her, and everybody got out of her way. The town folk knew who she worked for.

Then, tragedy struck our family. After ten years of working 18-hour days on business dealings, our father passed away at the age of 56 from a sudden illness. It was a hard time for our family. Dad wasn't even in the ground when relatives came out of the woodwork to pay their respects, and of course, trying to find a way to get their hooks into our family's fortune.

Our mom was no idiot, or anyone to mess with for that matter. She saw these greedy relatives coming long before they showed up knocking on our door. I was only nine at the time, but I remember hearing Mom reject offers from our relatives to take our family's money and double it or even triple it with some fly-by-night business ventures they were starting. Mom was candid when she responded to the relatives, "No, not interested, and don't ask again."

After months of trying to snuggle up next to our family, the relatives left us alone, kind of. Then rumors slowly started circulating that Mom was mentally unstable, a heavy drinker and had no business trying to raise a kid on her own. That type of gossip had some of our relatives curious, right along with the dollar signs that were popping in and out of their thoughts.

All their gossip was bullshit, and it was obvious to everyone that our relatives were just looking for a quick payday to support their lazy-ass lifestyles. Mom finally put an end to all the nonsense. She hired a lawyer and filed lawsuits against six of our relatives right along with their rumor mill and false accusations. The matter was instantly settled as their broke asses scrambled back into the woodwork to avoid being sued into oblivion by our family. We never heard from them again.

Mom was tough, straightforward, and she surprised the hell out of everyone when she started running Dad's businesses all on her own. She rolled up her sleeves and began making deals. She started more businesses and expanded our wealth by a considerable sum over the next few years. By the time I was fourteen, Mom had our family net worth sitting at nearly 9 million dollars, doubling what Dad had left us after his death. By this time, my two brothers had graduated college with degrees in business and then returned to help Mom run the company. To my surprise, they did well with the family business. They were naturals at running a company, just like our parents.

My brothers expanded our businesses by selling off some of our smaller businesses for a profit and opened a brokerage firm specializing in buying and selling cattle. They bought hundreds of acres where they raised several breeds of cattle and a few well-bred horses for show.

They also started a packing company wholesaling beef, and set up a transportation company to ship our meat from state to state. In addition to all the business deals, my brothers had a beautiful home built for the family on five hundred acres of land and we all lived there, including Ms. Birdie and Jeremiah. It was a nice place, beautifully designed and manicured with a swimming pool, gardeners, cooks, and housekeepers who took care of the twelve rooms in our ten thousand square foot home.

We were so rich. By the time I graduated high school in 1970, my family's wealth was sitting at nearly 50 million dollars thanks to Dad, Mom and my brothers. Our father would have been proud, maybe even a little jealous. My family had not made any bad business decisions, and the company they built grew by leaps and bounds. Hell, bankers damn near got into fistfights competing for our family's business. But our company was privately owned and operated and we didn't owe a cent to anyone. Mom paid cash for everything.

Then all eyes became focused on me and Jeremiah, Ms. Birdie's son. I was hounded by my brothers and my Mom to attend college and study law. My sister told them to leave me alone and to let me decide my own future. Scarlett was going through her own problems with Mom and needed me on her side, which I was. Scarlett and I were very close.

Well, I didn't want to attend college, and I didn't want to work for my family. Since I was a kid, I watched money rule our family, and all the discussions during dinnertime were about business and making more money. When Dad was alive we would pray at the dinner table every night, and business was never discussed. Dad focused on us kids and asked what we were up to at school, our grades, and our personal lives. But after he passed, the conversations turned to the talk of business, no prayers were said, and no one ever asked how I was doing.

Not to sound like the poor, spoiled little rich boy, but Mom and my brothers ignored me beyond belief. They were off building a fortune, working ungodly hours, and enjoying every minute of it, and Ms. Birdie primarily raised me. Of course, I had Jeremiah, who was more of a brother to me than my own brothers. Since Jeremiah and I were the same age, he and I did everything together: we hunted, we fished, we went to the same high school, double-dated, played baseball on the same team, and had our own pick-up trucks, which were our pride and joy. Basically, we partied our asses off and had a weekly allowance with which to do it. We were free to come and go as we pleased and no one bothered or questioned us in any way. But then we turned eighteen and we began to think for ourselves.

The day after graduation, Jeremiah and I were having a beer out by the swimming pool when the two of us came to a life-altering decision. We decided we wanted nothing to do with college or business, especially my family's business. We were serious and we made a decision right then, and stuck to it.

The next day we joined the Marine Corps on the buddy system. We also asked for service in Vietnam and a guarantee that we would be stationed together overseas. Our enlistment in the Marines was the perfect plan. I would watch his back and he would watch mine. We were brothers.

Unfortunately, not everything went as planned. When Jeremiah and I presented the news to our mothers, well, it didn't go over so well. Mom and Ms. Birdie were furious, which shocked the hell out of us. We thought they would be proud of us wanting to serve our country. With the simple snap of her fingers, Jeremiah and I were both considered outcasts for choosing the military over the family business. And my brothers yelled at me on a daily basis, threatening me with everything from poverty to death. But none of their bitching and moaning mattered. Jeremiah and I had already signed up for the Marines. It wasn't like we could change our minds and head off to college to fulfill our parent's dreams.

And my brothers blamed me for dragging Jeremiah along on my stupid scheme, as they called it. You see, Jeremiah and Ms. Birdie were family. They both lived at our house and it was well known that when Jeremiah graduated college, my brothers would set him up in a profitable position in the family's business.

So, when Jeremiah and I decided to enter the Marines, well, we were ostracized. No one- Mom, Ms. Birdie, or my brothers, would talk to either of us. To be honest, it really didn't matter that we were ostracized; Jeremiah and I had other shit to worry about, Southeast Asia for example.

After we graduated boot camp, Jeremiah and I thought all might be forgiven and the family would be proud of us, but they weren't. No one from the family wanted to see us. My oldest sister was the only member of the family I had any contact with. She, too, had left the family, and married a guy, which Mom didn't approve of, naturally.

Scarlett began building her own life and mother didn't like that. Scarlett was a certified accountant and happily married to a successful lawyer. The two had a wonderful life and two beautiful girls, who were not named after characters from "Gone with the Wind." But like me, Scarlett lived her life outside the love and acceptance of our family, and the family money, which neither of us would ever see. That's the way Mom wanted it. And Mom always got what she wanted.

The last time I spoke to Mom was the day I left for boot camp at the end of May 1970. And later when I was overseas, Mom refused to take my calls on her birthday or holidays. She would not acknowledge that I even existed. I wondered how she could do that. I just wanted to live life on my own terms, nothing more. I couldn't figure out why she was punishing me.

Mom passed away six years ago in 2007, and we hadn't spoken in over thirty-five years- and all because of money, and my departure from the family. The worse part was that she had control of the entire family estate, every cent of it. And to drive one last dagger through my heart, she made me the executor of her will. I knew the dirty details of the family business and where all the money was going.

After the funeral, I had to designate who would get what, how much, and to pass the bad news that the bulk of the family estate would be sold off and left to charity. Only a small fraction of the wealth went to family members. It was a nightmare. What was worse, I was the messenger, and according to my brothers and their wives, I was the bad guy. You should have seen the looks they gave me. This caused my brothers to hate me even more, because, in their eyes, it was me that made them poor.

Why Mom didn't leave the family business to our brothers

was a mystery to Scarlett and me. Chances are Mom had a falling out with Rhett and Brent before she passed. And when someone pissed off Mom, well, your ass was cut out of the will-forever. But in the end, my brothers weren't about to let Mom get away with selling off the company Dad had built, and in the process leaving them penniless. They got lawyers and began contesting the will, and Mom's sanity.

It didn't matter to me, though. Neither Scarlett nor I received a cent and we knew it going in. She and I still talk on a monthly basis but neither of us have anything to do with our brothers, their money-grubbing wives, or their lawyers. After the funeral, she and her husband moved to the Carolinas for his work. And I flew back to Colorado feeling like I had just won the lottery, glad to finally be putting the family, the money, and all the back stabbing out of my life.

But in the end, it would all come full circle and land right back in my lap, with brothers and lawyers circling trying to squeeze every nickel out of me that they could. By the way, my brothers are currently suing me.

Scarlett made a good point-she said that I was fighting two wars: one with my brothers and their lawyers, and my other war with PTSD due to Vietnam. And because of the two, my life would continue to be a nightmare. And she was right.

Well, that's it. That's my family, and how I joined the military and got to where I am today." I picked up my cold cup of coffee and took a sip.

Doctor Easton sat up straight in his chair and slowly leaned onto the armrest. He said nothing, but continued to look at me as if he were analyzing me with his eyes. He said, "Okay, hang on a second. I have a few questions here if you don't mind."

I said jokingly, "I thought you wanted the broad strokes about my family, how I grew up, but not the details?"

With a smile, Dr. Easton said, "Well, yeah, but shit, you can't leave me hanging here with so many loose ends about your family. If you don't mind, give me some details here, will you?

I responded, "Sure, ask away."

"Okay, first off, why in the hell were your brothers and their lawyers coming after you? You didn't receive any money; you only read the will, right? No, don't answer that. Let's go back farther. First, I want to know what happened to Ms. Birdie and Jeremiah after the two of you went into the Marines. You didn't mention anything about them."

"Well, I thought you wanted to talk about the military missions last?"

Doctor Easton said quickly, "Well, yeah, I do, but right now just give me the broad strokes, okay? Bring me up to speed here on how everything played out."

"All right, no problem, doc. Well, Jeremiah and I graduated boot camp and then went straight to our training school for nuclear, biological and chemical warfare. We were then sent to the Philippines for briefing and training and stayed there before he received orders for Vietnam.

There, Jeremiah and I were separated. I was being assigned to a Navy Lt. Commander in the Philippines; I'd be his assistant inspecting nuclear weapons. I often wondered what a nuclear weapon was doing in Vietnam in the early 1970's, but we were getting one and they named it 'Motherload.'

Jeremiah on the other hand, was what they called a chemical specialist, and I'll bet you can't guess where they assigned him in January 1971? They placed Jeremiah working with

'Agent Orange', you know, that chemical shit they sprayed in the jungles to kill all the foliage. Well, that shit kills more than foliage.

Anyway, to make a long story short, thirty-five years to the day of arriving in Vietnam, Jeremiah died of cancer in January 2006. He had cancer throughout his body-it was in his prostate, his liver, his lungs, his lymph nodes, his throat, and up and down his spine. And he was blind in one eye and weighed about 100 pounds, if that.

Hell, I didn't even know he was ill. Jeremiah and I would talk on the phone five or six times a year, but he never mentioned that he was sick. Hell, he sounded fine to me. No one called me, no one wrote me, not even Ms. Birdie. The way I heard about it was that Scarlett bumped into Ms. Birdie one day at the bank and the two got to talking. There, Scarlett found out that Jeremiah was dying due to his exposure to Agent Orange over in Vietnam. She immediately called me, and I dropped everything and flew back to the South to be with my best friend and brother.

Jeremiah passed away about an hour before my flight landed. I never got a chance to say goodbye. At his funeral I saw and talked to Ms. Birdie for the first time in over thirty-five years. She hugged me, kissed me and we had a chance to catch up- she still called me her brown-eyed-baby doll. It was at that point I could tell she forgave me for taking her son away from her.

No one from our family, my Mom or my brothers, came to Jeremiah's funeral, except Scarlett and me. I guess they were too busy making money and working their eighteen-hour days. After the funeral I stayed with Scarlett and her husband for two weeks. There I had a chance to catch up on the family business, and the gossip about my brothers and how their greedy-ass wives were spending them into oblivion.

Then the year 2007 rolled around and if you remember, that was the year Mom passed away. Then a year after that, I began to notice some changes within me. That was when my Post Traumatic Stress began to surface steadily. I was never the same after that. I have been struggling with it for some six years now, and it seems to be progressing. And now, here I am sitting across from you, telling you my life story and complaining about my troubles at work."

Doctor Easton said calmly, "Hang on a second. What about Ms. Birdie?"

I smiled slightly and said, "I could have gone the rest of my life without you asking that question, doc. Well…"

Doctor Easton sat up quickly and said, "Wait a second. I figured it out. Well, I think I've figured it out. Anyway, go ahead, tell me what happened."

I knew this doctor was smart. He not only listened to my story, but he also listened between the lines. That's not something you pick up in the civilian world, either, that's military training. I was quite sure he had figured it out. Anyway, I thought for a second and said, "I didn't really want to bring you this far into the darkness of my family, but I'll give you grand finale.

A year or two before Mom died from her cancer, she had rewritten her last will and testament with her lawyers, three in all, and spelled out what her wishes were after her death. Here's how it played out. Out of the 20 million dollars left in the family, Mom gave one million dollars to be divided between my two brothers. That was all they received, not a penny more.

My guess is they really did piss Mom off. Because at one point I heard the family fortune was valued at well over 120 million, but someone damn near ruined the company. So, someone screwed up, somewhere, and lost almost 70% of the company's value. The 20 million Mom was dishing out in her will was from the sale of the company, which went to her favorite charity. That's what our brothers were told, anyway."

Doctor Easton quickly said, "The money went to Ms. Birdie, right?" I knew Dr. Easton was a thinker.

I replied, "Oh yeah, but that's not the end of the story. In Mom's explicit instructions, Ms. Birdie was given our family home to use in taking care of Jeremiah. The house was Ms. Birdies to do with as she pleased. And in addition to that nice home, Mom set up Ms. Birdie with a monthly retirement income of $3,000 for life.

Now, here is where it gets a little tricky. Upon the death of Ms. Birdie, Mom's lawyers were then instructed to transfer the full amount to me. Once I receive the money, I am to split what's left, around $18 million, with Scarlett. But no money was to be given to either of my brothers."

"Wait a minute, when did you find all this out?"

"About an hour before I was to read the will. I was in the back of the law offices having coffee with Mom's lawyers when they decided to let me in on the money's final destination. After Mom's funeral I spent a few days with Scarlett and filled her in on what would happen after Ms. Birdie passed.

"Why wait to give you the money after Ms. Birdie passed? What's up with that?"

"I don't have the slightest idea. Scarlett thought that Mom was just evil in her old age, and wanted the two of us to see what we could have, but couldn't have, and how little we were getting, after all the family did have. The way

Scarlett and I saw it, if it didn't have malice attached, Mom wouldn't be interested in doing it. At least, that's our take on it.

"When did you get the money?"

"What money? I haven't received a penny."

"What, you're kidding!"

"I'm not joking. First, Ms. Birdie was born in 1916 and is still alive and well at the age of 97 years old. And she's in tip-top physical condition. She's thin; she eats really well, walks two miles a day, works in her garden, and drinks a bottle of red wine every night before she goes to bed. She's been doing that since Jeremiah and I were kids. Actually, Scarlett and I think Ms. Birdie will likely live to be well over 100 years old, maybe even to 110- you never know. That woman shows no signs of slowing down. But that's okay. She's earned a nice long life after all the years she had to put up with my family's shit.

Recently, Scarlett and I were informed by Mom's lawyers that our brothers, Rhett and Brent, somehow figured out that Mom left a portion of the money to Scarlett and me. Somebody talked and now our brothers were hovering, looking to get their hands on the entire amount. They wanted all the money and couldn't care less if Scarlett and I received a penny. My brothers and their wives had become accustomed to a certain lifestyle, and now they're broke. They weren't about to have that shit.

Fortunately, in spite of the recent lawsuits, threatening phone calls, and the private investigators, Mom's lawyers' countersued to get them off our back. So far, so good, but we'll see. At this point I don't trust my brothers or their wives to be anywhere near Ms. Birdie. Around my sister-in-laws, Ms. Birdie's a marked target and those bitches don't take prisoners, because money is their god. "

"Why would your mom do this to her children, you know, pit you all against each other scraping around for money?"

"I don't know, doc. Scarlett and I talked about it. We think that since Mom was dying, she wanted the four of us tearing out each others throats in some shape or form- some legacy, huh?"

Dr. Easton said with a concerned voice, "Hell, I'm worried about poor Ms. Birdie. You think she'll be okay?"

"I'm sure she'll be fine. She has a cousin living with her, and the house has an advanced security system, and there's always someone around during the day. And Ms. Birdie has herself an eighty-year-old man that visits from time to time. Ms. Birdie tells me she's a cougar."

Dr. Easton laughed out loud and then asked, "What'll happen to that big house once Ms. Birdie passes?"

"I'm not sure. If she gives us the house in her last will and testament, I told Scarlett to keep it and pass it on to her kids. Of course Ms. Birdie might give the house to her cousin. That's her last living relative. I have never met the woman but if Ms. Birdie trusts her, I trust her."

"So, that's why your brothers swamped you with lawsuits? I've never understood greed, especially where family is concerned."

"Well, doc, it's alive and well in our family. You only need to spend a couple days with my brothers and their wives to get a whole new education on greed and corruption."

"It must be nice, though, knowing you will be a millionaire- any idea what you might do with your share of the money?"

"Oh, I think about it from time to time, assuming Ms. Birdie doesn't outlive me. First, after Ms. Birdie passes, there'll be her funeral expenses, taxes on the inheritance and lawyers to pay once we get the money. I can't imagine how much all that'll cost or how much will be left. Second, I'll take care of Ms. Birdie's cousin, Haddie, assuming she outlives Ms. Birdie and wants to remain in the house. Then I plan on setting my kids up with enough money to do something, but not enough money to do nothing with their lives.

Well, that's about it. I can't think of anything else that pertains to the family. So, now you know all my family history, where do we go from here?"

Doctor Easton laughed out loud, stood up, stretched his back and said, "We still have your PTSD, work issues and military to get to today. Let's take a fifteen-minute break. We both could use some fresh coffee and I'm sure you're ready for a cigarette or two. Hell, after hearing about your family, I might need a cigarette, and I don't even smoke."

After twenty minutes both Doctor Easton and I returned to the conference room freezing our butts off. He had joined me outside for my third cigarette and the temperature had definitely dropped. Once we took our seats, Dr. Easton said with a shaky voice, "Okay, let's get started again. Why don't we take this time to have you tell me about your PTSD and how it affects you daily. Why don't we start with some of the issues you've been having lately and how you have handled it?"

Chapter Five - At Deaths Door

I leaned back on the couch and looked up at the ceiling, thinking. I didn't know where to start. With all the trouble I'd had over the previous months, not to mention the horrible thoughts running through my mind, well, that was enough to fill the doctor's legal pad. Thinking for a second, I began with the first thing that came to mind.

"All right, well, let's see. To start off with, I constantly worry about death, especially where my daughter and I are concerned. For some reason, I can't shake the thoughts that plague my mind on a daily basis. From day to day the fear of death is a faithful companion of mine, which is more of a burden than an asset. And I'm always on the alert thinking that everything and everyone around me is a threat. I'm always thinking about death and dying. Why, I have no idea.

When I'm at home I have it buttoned down tight. Every door is locked, and I double-check them several times a day, just to be sure. Each of my sliding windows in the house have a thick stick wedged firmly against the window and the frame to ensure no one can pry open the window from the outside. Each of my doors have double deadbolt locks and I have sensor lights set up all around the house with a warning alarm on the inside to alert me should anyone unauthorized get too close to the house. And if anybody does...it's their ass. I shit you not!

At night, I'm a very light sleeper. The slightest noise wakes me up. Regardless if I sense danger from the noises I hear or not, my fear compels me to get up, arm myself, and go downstairs. There, I cautiously investigate the disturbance, thinking that someone is trying to break into my home.

After a thorough search where I find nothing wrong, I slip back into bed, but can't get to sleep as I lay there wide awake thinking of what I might have missed. From that point on till daybreak, my mind is constantly alert, listening for the next noise that will send me downstairs peering though my Venetian blinds looking for the bad guys. I never seem to find any bad guys in my house, but you never know, there's a first for everything.

And let me tell you, I'm well armed and prepared for anything out of the ordinary. I have an M-14, 7.62MM rifle with two hundred rounds of ammunition and a sawed-off shotgun with plenty of shells. And I have a .45 caliber pistol with two nine round clips, and one of them strapped to the back of my headboard ready and half cocked. I also have several K-Bar knives strategically placed around the house that no one can see. Oh, and I have night vision gear and that shit's expensive and hard to get. But I know a guy... Doctor Easton, my perimeter is secure. If anyone fucks with my daughter, or me they die, I shit you not. And I don't take prisoners."

Doctor Easton asked, "What about outside the house, away from home, does that affect you?"

Thinking for a second, I answered, "Yeah, you bet it does. When I leave the house, I first check the surrounding area to make sure no one is lurking around. I'm always on the side of caution. To me, every car is a threat and every person is the enemy looking for an opportunity to take me out. When I'm out in public, which isn't all that often, I'm not far from the exits and I constantly have an eye on all the people coming and going. Why I do this, I have no idea, and let me tell you, it's exhausting.

If I'm in a restaurant, it's imperative that I sit where I have a clear view of everyone in the room. To me, they're all a threat, and no one is above suspicion, even the people in the back cooking or the wait staff. I trust no one. The reason I sit near the exits is in case something happens; my daughter and I will have a clear and safe exit while everyone else in the place is trying to figure out what is happening. You know, if some ass-wipe starts shooting, then I can shield my daughter while making a quick exit." I look at Doctor Easton, slightly shrug my shoulders and then pick up my coffee cup.

Doctor Easton said, "Sounds like you might have a touch of claustrophobia and be hyper-vigilant as well. What do you think?"

"I think I have a touch of both. The best I can tell is that I am claustrophobic, which for me carries its own punishments. Here, let me give you an example. When I'm at the grocery store, my daughter usually goes with me to run interference. She walks in front of my cart, graciously forcing people out of the way so they don't crowd me, which would otherwise cause me to have an anxiety attack and force me to leave the store. It's difficult for my daughter, but she doesn't care how many people she pisses off as long as I am not cornered or put in some stressful situation. She has seen me at my worst and will definitely step in and help when necessary. She has been a great support and I can't ask any more of her than that."

Doctor Easton asks, "What's so bad for you in the stores-the open space, or the people?"

"Yeah, it can be the people, especially if it's too busy. But most of the time I tend to stress when I need to get something down one of the aisles. I try not to go down the aisles because it's too narrow, and the narrow aisles remind me of entering the back of a helicopter, which can stir up a whole new set of anxieties for me. That's why I take my daughter with me to the store. I tell her what I need and she gets it. Hell, I even develop an anxiety attack when in my car. There, my troubles come if I'm caught in a traffic jam for any period of time and several cars have me locked in the middle lane. By the time I get where I'm going, I'm mentally and physically drained, not to mention on high alert and not in a very good mood."

Doctor Easton said, "You really care about that daughter, don't you?"

"Oh yeah, regardless of my claustrophobia and security issues, a lot of the time my mind is occupied toward the well-being of my daughter. I'm so afraid that something might happen to her. When she's out with her friends and fails to call home or check in with me on a regular basis, I immediately go into panic mode. I think to myself-why hasn't she called? Why isn't she answering her cell phone? I'll bet she had an accident. I'll bet she was killed and a cop is on his way to the house right now to tell me about it. How will I handle the news, and who is responsible for her death? I will be taking a giant shit on someone, Marine Corps style. Hell, she might have even been kidnapped and I wasn't there to protect her. Why do I let her hang out with all her friends? I think sometimes that I am only thinking of myself and that makes me a lousy parent.

Then, finally, when she calls or arrives home safely, I feel like a ton of weight has lifted off my shoulders. Calmly I tell her, "Sweetie, you have to tell Dad where you are, I get worried about you." She knows that I suffer from Post Traumatic Stress and that I freak out when I'm not in control of every situation. She tells me that she gets wrapped up in conversation with her friends and forgets to call. And hell, can you blame her? If I were her, I wouldn't want to be thinking about me, either. Hell, I don't like thinking about me...and I'm me.

Recently, she received her driver's license, and even though she's an excellent driver, my stomach's in a constant knot when she's out of the house in her SUV. For example, when Casi's not at home and I happen to hear the siren from an ambulance or police car, I freak out and phone her, thinking she's been in a major accident and needs my help. And as usual, I can't reach her by phone. Then I am a nervous wreck, pacing around the house humming the Marine Corps Hymn to myself as a way to give me confidence and comfort.

Frantically, I sit on my couch pulling at my hair, eating my fingernails, or I walk around the house with horrible thoughts running through my head that an ambulance is on the scene trying to pull her free from the twisted metal of a car accident. I think to myself, those damn foreign vehicles are made of aluminum foil. She needs her father, and I am not fucking there. And what really sucks is that I hear sirens at least a couple of times a day. When I call my daughter's cell phone for no apparent reason, and if I get lucky and she answers, she always asks, "Dad, did you hear sirens again?"

In a concerned voice, Doctor Easton asked, "I know you love your daughter and her safety ties up a lot of your time, mentally, but do you ever worry about your own health?"

Chapter Six - Health Issues

"Do I ever worry about my own health? Hell, that's an understatement. Every time I have a turd cross ways in me, I'm off to the doctor's office for a checkup, thinking that I have prostate or colon cancer. When my back hurts for a few days in a row, negative thoughts began to run through my head. With that pain, I think cancer has developed in my back or one of the rods or screws I have implanted have slipped out of place. Every ache or simple pain catches my attention.

But as a hypochondriac, whenever I visit my doctor, and after he runs a few tests, he assures me that all my worrying was for nothing. Then when I develop a bad headache, I'm back in his office complaining that I may have a brain tumor or I'm about to have a stroke. Fuck, I've been so worried; I've actually talked my doctor into sending me in for a CAT scan. He reluctantly agrees and off I go to a specialist.

Over the past year, I've been to the doctor's office so much, everyone from the doctors to the secretaries know me by my first name, and I get Christmas cards from their office every year. So, I've tried not to visit the doctor every time I have the smallest ache or pain, because my doctor always tells me there's nothing wrong, and then sends me home. I really try not to worry, but it's hard. I'm so afraid that something will happen to me and my daughter will have to grow up without a father. I need to stay healthy and alert. I trust no one else to raise her.

Unfortunately, my worrying about every little pain managed to backfire on me, in a reverse sort of way. A few months ago my back hurt so bad that I thought it was going to kill me. For eight hours I rolled around on the couch and floor telling myself that it was all in my head and I would be fine in a little while. When I finally couldn't take the pain anymore I dragged myself, limping, into my doctor's office. He examined me, did an ultrasound on my back and side, and discovered that I had a kidney stone. It was serious enough that my doctor put me in the hospital for three days to control not only my pain but my stress level as well. You see, I'm damned if I do, and I'm damned if I don't."

Once he had taken several notes, Doctor Easton looked up and said, "Gary, let's go back to the claustrophobia for a minute. If you don't mind, I want to know how it affects you from day-to-day."

"Okay, I'll do the best I can." Scratching my head I said, "Well, as I said a minute ago, I believe claustrophobia is one of my biggest problems. I definitely have trouble getting on an elevator, being in a building with more than one floor, or in an area with a large group of people. It's not that I think the elevator will fall to the basement, it's just that there's no room in one of those things, especially when it opens and there are ten other turds standing inside the elevator waiting for me to get on. Fuck that! I take the stairs, back pain or not.

And as far as tall buildings are concerned, I'm afraid that if a fire breaks out, I'd be trapped with no exit. Let's be reasonable, if you were in a tall building, doc, and a fire did break out, what the fuck would you do? Would you go to the roof or take the stairs down? Thinking like me, what floor would you want the hotel to put you on?

Hell, I don't take any chances. I can't afford to. Whenever I'm out of town on business I have a room on either the first or second floor, which I set up well in advance. If a fire breaks out, I figure that I can easily jump twenty to thirty feet to safety. I believe it is better to break a leg than cook to death in a stairwell. You know what I mean?

Shit! I hate tight places. When I'm at work and wedged in my small office, people are always coming around for one reason or another, which makes me feel like the walls are closing in around me. When that happens my heart begins to race, my breathing is rapid and short, and I feel smothered. I find it hard to breathe, my vision becomes blurry, and my skin feels as if it's being torn from my body. My head starts to hurt, I become dizzy, and I can't get out of the room and the building fast enough without drawing too much attention to myself."

Dr. Easton asked, "Have you always had this, or has it developed since the military?"

"I'm not sure. I never felt this way as a kid, or while I was in the Marines for that matter. It has to have something to do with my tour overseas."

In a curious tone, Doctor Easton asked, "What do you think could have caused it, any ideas?"

"Actually, doc, I've given that some thought. The best guess I can give is that during the Fall of Saigon, our security forces there were constantly under the threat of being overrun by the refugees. When we had a thousand of refugees on the island at one time, gangs would form, the refugees got out of hand, their attitudes would flare, which put us all on high alert because we were outnumbered a hundred and fifty to one, and that was just in the beginning, and it was like that for months.

The refugees definitely knew the odds were stacked in their favor, and because of that, they were constantly trying to see how far they could push us before we reacted. We were always on a constant state of alert and when necessary, we reacted. We always had the upper hand because we were well-armed and they knew my Marines were not about to take any of their shit. It was like they knew how far to push us before they knew to pull back and disperse. And from first hand experience, they knew what it took to piss me off.

Other than blaming my problems on the refugees, the claustrophobia could have been caused due to the amount of time I spent in the jungle in Asia. It wasn't unusual for our nine-man patrol to be in the jungle for days at a time where we were constantly surrounded by the thick foliage of the jungle. Sometimes you couldn't see six feet in front of you.

When in the jungle, each of us lived with the threat that enemy soldiers could be only be a few feet away and we'd never know it. Shit, in a jungle war, it's always a stressful situation. You never know who has the upper hand. And doc, as far as my claustrophobia is concerned, I always felt like the jungle was closing in around me. That might be the cause; I'm not sure, just saying."

In a concerned voice, Dr. Easton asked, "Your youngest daughter still lives with you, correct?"

Surprised that he asked that, I replied, "Yeah, she lives with me. It's been just the two of us now for the last seven years."

Doctor Easton said, "Sounds like the two of you are getting along okay, I mean, considering?"

I answered, "We do. She is the best part of me and I would do anything to keep her safe."

"Yeah, I know you would. But remember the other day on the phone when I called to tell you about this meeting? Remember that day I asked you what were some of the things that were troubling you the most? And you mentioned losing interest in everything, work, hobbies, life in general, and how everything seemed to be closing in surrounding you? Yeah, I'd like to know what that's about."

Chapter Seven - Lack of Interest

Thinking for a second I said, "Yeah, I remember our conversation now. Well, I've lost interest in my job for sure, the people I work with, and anything that used to mean something to me. I'm not talking about my kids or anything like that; just the outside forces working against me, especially shit that bores me. I don't know when it actually started but the best I can tell a numbness came over me gradually, saw what it liked, and decided to stay. There's something deep inside of me, which has sent my emotions into the proverbial tailspin where nothing excites me anymore, not even sex. Work doesn't excite me, nor does working out, which I used to love, especially jogging. I also have no interest in dating or relationships and all those around me can see it.

I dated for about three months after my divorce but due to a lack of interest, I eventually cut her loose and haven't been with a woman since. It's been six years since I have had sex with a woman and I haven't missed it in the least. Actually, I show about as much interest in relationships as a pig would about roller skates. As I said, I couldn't care less. It's like I'm emotionally numb all over. There's nothing that excites me in life. I hate my past, I hate the present, and as far as I'm concerned, I have nothing to look forward to in the future except for the safety and success of my youngest daughter. That's actually the only positive outlook I have is my daughter. She's my baby."

Doctor Easton asked, "What do you mean that you feel numb? Does that have something to do with your back injury?"

"No, my back problems are a different story all together, but I'll get to that later."

Doctor Easton then said, "Well, I'm still not getting a picture of what you're describing."

"Well, simply put, things that normally get people excited, I don't have. Here, let me give you an example. When my mother passed away, my daughter and I flew back to the South for the funeral. When my brothers and sister first saw our mother lying in the casket, my siblings became distraught and overcome with emotions, which is normal for grieving family members. But I never flinched, blinked, grimaced, or shed a tear for that matter.

Actually, I couldn't have cared less. I showed more emotion when I had friends killed overseas than I did when I saw my own mother lying in a casket. Because of my lack of emotions, my brothers and sister thought I was very cold and uncaring. Of course, my brothers commented that I was only trying to hide my emotions, and that wasn't healthy. They are always trying to give me advice, whether I like it or not. I'm the youngest in the family and they think they know what is best for me. They don't understand that I couldn't care less.

Of course, they don't have any fucking idea what they're talking about, and I've never told them about being diagnosed with PTSD or my back being broken. And I wasn't about to try and explain my disease to a room full of people who don't need to know, or wouldn't understand if I told them. It's a Marine thing, they just wouldn't understand."

Doctor Easton asked, "Was that the first time you noticed the problem with your emotions?"

Chapter Eight – Emotions

"That was the first time. And even though I loved my mother dearly, I loved the people I served with in the military more. In retrospect, too many of my fellow Marines died horrible deaths and had their young lives cut short through no fault of their own. Hell, some of my troops were killed at the age of eighteen and nineteen and many of them had pregnant wives or infants back home.

Over the years when I've listened to civilians try to give their explanation as to why we were in this war or that war, I always hear the same thing. To most civilians we were just young, stupid kids with one foot in the grave who didn't know any better or we would not have joined the military in the first place. I hate that fucking kind of talk, especially from those pricks who have not served. They have big mouths, narrow minds and make uneducated statements.

But I'm here to assure you that our Marines were well trained, dedicated, loyal, and would have gladly given their lives in the service of their country. My Marines are far better than any of these knee-jerk fuck-heads I've had the displeasure to meet in this civilian shit. These Marines are real men who risked their lives so others may live. They risk their lives by volunteering for dangerous assignments where they always put others first, themselves last, and all for the good of the mission. doc, you cannot put a price on that type of loyalty. And I resent any sloppy ass sissy civilian piece of shit who comments otherwise. As a matter of fact, I would rather send one of them into the shit for a day and let them experience it for themselves instead of trying to explain it to them. Let's see what kind of attitude they have then.

Now, years later, I look back and remember their lives, their faces, and how they made the ultimate sacrifice. Because of those memories, I feel guilty. I often ask myself why I lived and others died. The memories of my friends, which are the only real family I've really ever known are in my thoughts every day.

So, when I saw my mother dead and lying in a casket, it didn't faze me in the least. Actually, during the funeral services, I kept looking at my watch to see how much time we had left before we could leave and hit the pub."

I paused for a moment as I had images of my fellow Marines dancing around in my head. I caught myself staring off at the walls, and then turned to Doctor Easton and continued.

"Then, several months after the funeral, my condition seemed to worsen and then I noticed something. When my daughter wrapped her arms tightly around my body to give me a big hug, I felt nothing inside. Of course, I could feel the pressure of her arms around me, but not the overflow of feeling and excitement I once had whenever she wanted to give her dad a hug.

For the benefit of my daughter, of course I made a big deal about the hug and returned an emotion-free hug back to her. My daughter couldn't tell the difference, but I could. Of all the crap I've had to put up with because of my PTSD, I knew something new was surfacing within my mind, which would definitely take me into a horrifying direction and fuck with me for years to come. I had to sit and think about my lack of emotions at that point.

Think about it for a second. When I couldn't feel a hug from my daughter, well, that fucked with me for awhile and kept me up at night making me wonder, what does this disease have in store for me next?"

Doctor Easton said, "It's obvious you are carrying around a lot of internal stress. So does your PTSD surface when you're just under stress, or around a large group of people, or both?"

Chapter Nine - Stress

"Since I have no idea what will come out of my mind, or my mouth for that matter, from day-to-day, I've been under a lot of stress because of these unexpected visits of unknown and, of course, unexamined thoughts. Most of the time at work, it's like I'm walking around in a haze, you know, like a dream where you don't know if you're really awake or still dreaming.

Sometimes, it's hard to tell the difference between a dream and reality. I forget things I was doing or was supposed to do and I usually bump into shit throughout the course of the day and that snaps me back to reality. For some reason I seem to be okay when I am driving to and from work. And sometimes I don't even remember the trip to and from work.

Sometimes, at my desk, I'll be working on something important and then stop to balance my checkbook. After a few minutes of being engaged in adding and subtracting, I'll ask myself, why the fuck did I do that? Regardless of what I'm working on, my mind wanders off into the unknown, which will force me to stop what I'm doing and start on something else. Hell, I can only tell you about it, I can't explain it.

My mind wanders so much that it reminds me of someone changing the channel within my mind. One minute I'm at my desk thinking about an issue at work, the next second, my mind switches and I'm thinking about a problem my daughter is having with one of her teachers. Then, out of nowhere, my mind will shift to horrible memories I experienced in the Marines, which stirs up horrible demons that seem to take on a life of their own. When that happens, my attitude changes and it's not good for anyone to be around me asking a bunch of stupid questions or talking about mundane shit like the carpet they just bought or tricks their fucking dog can do.

This unknown demon seems to force vivid memories of my past to resurface with such clarity that it is sometimes hard to distinguish between past and present. On more than one occasion, I thought I was losing my mind. I just could not hold my thoughts together. And when I experience this mental meltdown, a panic attack is most likely to follow. It's so frustrating that I'm lucky to make it through a full day without screaming and running naked across the campus.

Since I have no control over what enters and exits my mind, I continue to get nervous when people get too close to me, which makes me feel surrounded and insecure. I break out in a sweat and my hands start to shake, and I become nauseated. Because of what I have to endure during the day, at night, I began having nightmares, problems sleeping, and at every turn the walls were closing in on me. I feel trapped, alone, and afraid. I try to take my mind off the random thoughts by thinking about what my daughter and I would be doing over the weekend.

It doesn't matter where I am, whether at home, work or at a shopping mall with my kid, whenever I feel cornered or stressed, I mentally slip from peaceful reality to that parallel universe in my mind where things are not so pleasant. In that unhappy state, it forces my attitude to change from calm and reasonable, to one of hate, distrust, and mostly anger. I seem to blame everyone but me.

Anytime I feel threatened or cornered, I will somehow mentally switch into a psychological profile that makes me unpredictable, moody and sometimes dangerous. When I'm in this state of mind, I can't tolerate my boss or my coworkers, and since I cannot trust anyone, I'm always suspicious that someone's out to hurt me or sabotage my career.

Whatever caused this problem to surface wasn't just limited to my stress at work or the people around me. Anytime I'm in a tight spot such as a store, a mall, church, or any place where I have to be around a large group of people, I began to have difficulty breathing. I start sweating and become very agitated. Before long, I lose my temper and have an anger outburst, which forces me to leave because I have no idea how I will react when I'm out of my comfort zone. And people at work tend to avoid me whenever possible due to the look on my face or my aggressive looking posture. My boss, Steve, who happens to be one of the good guys, when he sees me coming with that look on my face he says, "At ease, Sarge, at ease." He is just joking and I am fine with him saying anything to me because we actually get along.

It's especially bad when I'm in a team meeting at work. There I'm usually in a small meeting area and the room fills up with twenty to thirty people. I then begin to sweat, get jumpy, and worst of all I feel as if every person in the room has their eyes upon me.

I can only stand about five minutes of being surrounded before I excuse myself for a bathroom break. But in reality, I'm off to get a cup of coffee and then outside for a cigarette. Once I'm outside I breathe better, I'm more relaxed, and it takes me a good twenty minutes of walking around before I can re-enter whatever environment caused my setback. And when I'm not at the team meetings you can bet your ass that management notices my absences. My boss, Steve, suspects something is up with me, but just gives me a nod but never asks probing questions.

Now, anyone in their right mind will tell you there's no

threat in a team meeting, and most people would agree with you, except me. But I'm here to tell you that it doesn't matter where I am or what I'm doing, I feel immediately threatened, claustrophobic, panicked, and that usually causes an anxiety attack to surface.

I'm not sure how much more of this shit I can take. I've been struggling with this crap for years and to tell you the truth, I don't see any light at the end of the tunnel. My problems have gotten worse over the years, and they're constantly compounding, which only creates more stress for me to deal with.

It's been months since I first sought help from the other Veteran's Center up north, and I'm not any closer to getting well than the day I walked through that door. As a matter of fact, I'm worse off now than when I first started therapy. That's why I came here to see you. Now I'm not blaming the VA by any means, it's just that my progress has been slow, if there is progress at all. And now with all my troubles at work and other things that have been happening to me, it's causing all the stress to pile up on me, squeezing me into an unknown abyss of mental darkness. And in that darkness, I am all alone, stumbling around in the darkness of my mind looking for the light.

Over the past few months my panic attacks have increased, and when one strikes, I feel like I'm at deaths door. And as you know, it's a sudden horrible force that comes over me, mimicking that of a heart attack letting me know that I am about to die and my daughter will grow up a fucking orphan.

When it starts, I have trouble breathing, I begin to sweat profusely, and my mid-section feels as if a belt is squeezing the life out of me. But the most horrible feeling is when it seems that millions of pins are pushing from the inside trying to get out. When one of these attacks comes I have to leave the store or my office to go outside and walk around until it dissipates. And that's the bitch about an anxiety attack. They come on fast and seem to last for an eternity, twenty to thirty minutes before they subside, but occasionally they last longer. A second can seem like a minute, and a minute can seem like an hour.

I'm not sure what brings them on most of the time. Sometimes when I hear a baby crying, or I get startled in some way, a little while later, an attack will soon follow. Whenever I hear a balloon pop, a car backfire, or a door slam it startles me, which causes a hundred thoughts to run through my head, and they're not pleasant thoughts. Sometimes I get anxiety attacks and don't know why. Currently, I have about three attacks a day, and they're playing hell on my mental stability not to mention my dealings with those around me."

Doc Easton shifted in his seat, took a sip of coffee and asked, "Are you sleeping any better than the last time we saw each other, or are you still having those nightmares you were telling me about?"

Chapter Ten - Nightmares

Thinking for a moment I answered, "At night I sometimes fall asleep, but most of the time I can't. I go to bed early, around eleven or twelve o'clock, but all I do is toss and turn until the wee hours of the morning. On the nights I finally manage to fall asleep, it's usually around three or four in the morning, which is a bitch because I have to be up at six to get my daughter up for school. And worse yet, I have to be at work by eight. Can you imagine what the rest of my day is like? If you think that's bad, you should see me on the nights when I have the nightmares you were speaking of.

In the past I didn't have nightmares every night, but lately I seem to be. Most nights I just lie in bed afraid to go to sleep for fear of what's going to surface because of it. In my nightmares, something always seems to be chasing me trying to kill me. And when I wake, the nightmare has scared the shit out of me. And there is no going back to sleep after that. I might as well go down stairs and make coffee."

Doc Easton asked, "What do you mean chasing you, what's chasing you?"

"I think its death chasing after me, doc, but I'm too busy running to turn and have a good look. In the dream I'm usually in a burned out building or on some twisted, rusted metal structure of some kind. I'm running away, too afraid to look at what's nipping at my heels. Most nights I dread going to sleep, too scared that whatever it is that's chasing me, will catch me, and then what? What happens if it catches me, do I die or just wake up? Either way, I don't want to know.

In other nightmares, I am climbing a beautiful white spiral staircase up through the clouds, and once at the top, I voluntary fall forward into the unknown vortex without a care in the world. But as I fall, it gets darker and then I began notice dead bodies lining the clouds on both sides of me. Some of the bodies are pointing toward the light below, which will eventually be my destination, while the other bodies are reaching through the clouds grabbing for me. I don't know if the dead are trying to slow my fall, or they're trying to drag me into their world. Regardless, the gravity in that nightmare keeps me from sticking around to find out. When I wake up I'm sweating, scared and shaking so bad that I can't even get out of bed. I just lie there.

Another nightmare is where my men and I are killed in combat. In that nightmare there are only a few of us on a mission when we come under fire and get wiped out. When I wake up and discover it was only a nightmare, I feel like a failure. For most of the day, the memory of the nightmare weighs heavy on my thoughts making me feel guilty, like I left some unfinished business behind because of my failed mission. That nightmare has been popping up a lot lately, but varies from time to time. Regardless, I awake sweating, shaking and scared as hell."

Doctor Easton asked, "Are you taking any sleeping medications, or are you using your pain meds to help you sleep?"

"Over the years I've taken various medications to fall asleep, but the next day I feel like shit, which is worse than not sleeping at all. The medication makes me so drowsy that it's hard for me to function during the day. For me, the pain pills have been pulling double duty, helping me to sleep at night and taking away some of the pain in my back. But still, it's no guarantee that I will get more than four hours a night, and that's assuming I don't hear any bad guys trying to break into the house. Hell, if one of our fish farts in the tank, I'm up for the rest of the night."

Doctor Easton laughed and said, "Let's go back to last week where we touched on some of the intrusive thoughts you were having."

Chapter Eleven - Deep Thoughts

"Well, I'm still not sure what intrusive thoughts are. But as a layman, I relate those thoughts to driving down the street and someone runs a red light and T-Bone's me. Sorry, but that's the best way for me to explain how these sharp mental images of the past somehow break in on my regular conscious thoughts and disrupt my normal thought patterns."

Doc Easton smiled and asked, "Got some examples?"

"Well, when I'm at work, suddenly, out of the corner of my right eye, I'll catch a brief glance of a helicopter coming straight for me with the blade spinning. Of course, it's only an image within my mind, but to me, that doesn't mean it isn't there. When I see images such as that, most of the time I jump, blink or flinch thinking I'm about to be hit by a crashing helicopter. When people see me flinch, twitch, or throw my arms into the air reacting to some image I'm responding to, they look all wide-eyed, freezing in their seat. I get asked, "Hey man, you okay?" I usually just respond with, "Yeah, I just nodded off for a second." Believe me, when these images appear and catch me off guard it's embarrassing as hell. And I don't like explaining myself to co-workers.

At other times various images of the military will interrupt my thought process, which will have my mind working overtime for days at a time. When I've been in team meetings or under stress, I spot images such as falling helicopters, or enemy soldiers stepping out of the jungle and stabbing at me with bayonets. At other times, I'll briefly see the faces of dead Marines that I once knew. Sometimes I flinch or just stare off in space trying to get a fix on what just happened to me. At home, images like that have sent me under my dining room table curled up in a ball with a blanket wrapped around me like a cocoon. I like it there. It comforts me for some reason."

Shaking his head, Doctor Easton looks up at me, smiles, and asks, "Gary, do you have any good days?"

Chapter Twelve - Good Days-Bad Days

"This may sound crazy but I have discovered something positive about myself in the midst of all this bullshit. I do love to be alone. Freedom is my most treasured value. Of all the things I could put first in my life, freedom is at the top of the list. I have family, friends and money, but nothing relaxes me more than being alone with no noise and my own thoughts. When I'm in that frame of mind, I seem to think clearly. I don't like noise at all, especially big trucks or motorcycles.

But here's something I think you may find interesting, doc. I truly enjoy going to the mountains on a snowy day. God, do I love that. Up there I have a special spot picked out where I sit on a large, tall rock meditating and listening to the snowfall. Did you know there is not a horn, a television, a radio, a child crying, or a siren heard up there? When it's really quiet outside, which it usually is in the mountains, you can actually hear the snowfall slowly hit the ground, or the sound of a hawk moving its wings as it passes close by. Damn. Those are the days I cherish the most. I guess if I had to get excited about anything, it would have to be that.

If for some reason I happen to pass away up there, it would be a good death. Think about this for a second. Can any of you think of a better way to exit this earth? I know that I can't. Compare a death like that to the thought of lying in a hospital rotting to death from some disease gnawing away at the internal parts of your body. Or dropping dead from a heart attack and having a team of people pumping on your chest. I don't know about you, but that's not a very appealing way to exit this life, if you know what I mean. For me, I want to die alone, in the mountains, on a snowy day, listening to snow gently hitting the ground. What a way to go, alone and own my own terms with no one around." I paused for a sip of coffee.

On the down side, probably the last thing I can think of that's troubling to me is the pain I experience on a daily basis. Not the mental pain mentioned earlier, but the physical pain from my lower back and legs. I'm sure you remember me mentioning how I broke my back while on active duty in the Marines. It happened on a search and rescue mission looking for survivors after a helicopter was shot down. But I am sure we will get to that in a bit.

Due to the extent of my injuries, I eventually had to have surgery, which only relieved about thirty percent of my pain. Currently, I have six screws and two rods holding me together back there. And on any given day the pain in my lower back can be so severe that I can hardly walk, or the pain will put me in bed for days at a time. If it is hot outside my back hurts, when winter sets in my back hurts, if I lose a few pounds my back really hurts.

During the normal course of a day, I can only stand for short periods, fifteen to twenty minutes at a time. When I'm sitting at work or lounging at home, the pain causes me to shift positions every few minutes or so. At other times, I have to stand up to relieve some of the aching. At night, the pain in my back wakes me up several times throughout the night, regardless if I'm having nightmares or not. For someone who has a full time job, this problem has played hell on my employment record over the years.

So, not only am I labeled with this mental disease, I also have the physical pain in my back to contend with as well. You tie these two together and it makes for one hell of a fucked-up individual just trying to survive in a cold, greedy, unwelcoming society in which I am not accepted. Out here in this environment, no one cares what you did for your country. They are only interested in getting the product out the door and talking about themselves."

Doctor Easton leaned back in his chair and placed his left foot on the edge of the table between us. He then asked, "What upsets you the most about being around people?"

Chapter Thirteen - Mental Meltdowns

"Well, sometimes I think its people in general who get on my nerves. I just tend to have a strong dislike for bossy people, or anyone who takes their job too seriously. I also hate pushy Christians who think the world should follow the written word of the Bible and all of the other bullshit they spew trying to control me or those around me. Then, there is the kiss-ass. Of all the people I despise, they are the worst. And when I'm in a public venue outside of work, crowds make me nervous, and regardless of where I'm at I try to get in and out as soon as possible to avoid having any contact with any of them."

Doctor Easton asked, "Give me some examples. Wait a second, what happened at that Christmas party you were at? We touched on it last time we met but I never heard the conclusion."

"Let's see. One evening last year, I was invited to a Christmas party with about twenty other people held by a close friend of mine. He, too, is a Veteran. During the Vietnam War he was a Corpsman, you know, like a paramedic in the civilian world, but far more advanced. Anyway, he had seen his share of death and destruction and because of his troubles adjusting to society, well, let's just say the two of us are really good friends with a lot in common.

Being a close friend, I had shared some of my experiences with him about my PTSD over a beer or two from time to time, and my problems with large groups of people and public settings. When he invited me he knew I would decline, but after a little nudging, I agreed to show up. Besides, my daughter thought it was a good idea for me to get out of the house. She thought it might do me some good to be out and around people other than those I worked with, but I had my doubts. But what the hell, I figured it couldn't be that bad. I would stay fifteen or twenty minutes and then leave. I was making an effort at least.

When I arrived at the party I pretty much kept to myself. But it wasn't long before people approached me to introduce themselves and strike up a conversation, which I skillfully managed to get out of. The group inside was mostly a bunch of dull boring people who talked of nothing more than their own self-importance, their jobs, or bad relationships.

Inside the party, I avoided anything that looked like a conversation. I stood there just counting the seconds until I could excuse myself and leave for the night without insulting my friend. From time to time I would see him look over at me, nod, and smile. He knew I was struggling, but he kept an eye on me. Grady was a good friend and the closer I got to him the safer I felt. Although I could see Grady struggling with the party as well, he patiently tried to work the room talking to everyone.

Trying not to be cornered, Grady and I worked our way around people and met up by the front door. I was so glad he and his wife had a nice large house with that big den. Grady enjoys my company and to tell you the truth, I think he'd rather spend time with me than having to entertain a room full of people. But he had to work the room to appease his wife, or pay the price, because most of the people there were her teaching friends or college administrative personnel. After a couple of minutes of talking to Grady, his wife motioned for him to meet her in the kitchen. There I was, alone with strangers once again.

While sipping my beer, I decided to take a breather and step outside for a cigarette. I'd only been at the party for five minutes or so. That particular night was bitter cold, but the crisp winter night air was a better companion than listening to the mundane chitchat taking place inside the house. I know that sounds pompous of me but what could I do?

Twenty minutes and two cigarettes later, I rejoined the party, positioning myself some distance from the others by pretending to notice Grady's video collection. He had a shit-load of documentaries, actually impressive. From time to time someone would wander over, smile and strike up some boring conversation about the weather or what not. When they ran out of things to say in their one sided conversations, they would become bored with me and move on to someone else who looked interested in their banality.

Personally, I couldn't care less what people talk about but why do I have to hear about it? But for the most part I tried to appear interested by smiling and nodding graciously, usually not paying much attention to their subject matter. While they talked I counted the rectangles in the painting on the wall behind them. I was never rude to anyone, I was always polite and appeared concerned about their subject matter.

While standing patiently listening to some guy talk about his golden retriever, a tall, lanky, overdressed man with a manicure named Stuart joined the two of us with about three drinks in him. Stuart moved around people at the party as if he were royalty, or at least wanted people to think he was somebody. And in addition to his well-groomed hair and manicure, every chance he had, Stuart tried to catch a glimpse of himself in anything that gave him a reflection. He was a phony and I hate phonies. Stuart was loud, condescending, and lacked the basic social skills as he talked of politics, religion, and education. Stuart continued giving everyone his narrow-minded view on how if he were in charge; America would be a better place to live. I fucking hate that kind of talk. I tried to avoid him all night, but there he was, standing only a few feet from me and talking loud, wanting to resonate throughout the crowd.

He was a legend in his own mind and thought he was the life of the party. Stuart was so full of himself that he waved over a few other people to join in his rhetoric, thinking others in the room would be interested in an uneducated view of government spending.

Reluctantly, I stood there listening to the idiot spout what I thought was a load of crap, until his topic of conversation switched from education to politics. And within minutes of making that subtle transition he had pissed me off beyond recognition and I was doing my best to stay quiet and not grind my molars down to the gums.

His subject matter was old news, as he carried on about how much it was costing him out of his own pocket to support the deadbeats in society who live in the lap of luxury off the U.S. Government's dime. He was persistent in telling us how the Democrats and their giveaway welfare systems were destroying the moral fiber of this country by setting such a bad example for future recipients.

The more he talked the louder he got, especially his laugh, and I'm sure the booze was a contributing factor to most of his bullshit. But when his opinion shifted from welfare to disabled veterans sucking the system dry, he had my full and undivided attention. I bit my lip and listened closely, trying not to draw any attention to myself.

His contention was that veterans are nothing more than glorified welfare recipients drawing government dollars for phony symptoms of a disorder called PTSD. He said that all the Post Traumatic nonsense was nothing more than veterans looking for another way to pick his pocket each month. He was adamant about getting a Republican elected to office to put the brakes on all the unnecessary spending, and put the lazy ass veterans back to work.

On the outside my hands began shaking and if you could have seen my face, I'll bet it was blood red. I couldn't believe what I was hearing. The man openly admitted he had no military experience, but he chose to judge veterans based on his limited knowledge of PTSD, not knowing what we have to go through just to be able to listen to assholes like him and not kill him. He definitely pushed the wrong buttons, and the bitch of it was that most of the people listening agreed with him as they nodded their heads or gave him a high-five… the sophomoric fuck. The more the jerk spouted, the more anxious I was to throw his happy ass through the window and then go out and piss in his mouth. I was seconds from making my move.

Having enough, I opened my mouth to enter the conversation, but before I could utter a word, a hand appeared on my shoulder, breaking my concentration. I glanced around to see my friend Grady, brushing past me staring at this bastard like he was about to snatch him up by the neck and alleviate the party of his presence. And I had my buddy's back. Grady heard the heart of the conversation and stepped over just at the right time.

Then, before Grady had a chance to tear Stuart a new asshole verbally, a well-dressed elderly gentleman, a retired college professor in fact, stepped forward and read Stuart the riot act about boasting on that about which he had no knowledge. The older gentleman was calm but had a deep voice that resonated throughout the crowd. He told Stuart that anyone making less than a million dollars a year had no business voting for a Republican, and that Stuart didn't look like he made a million dollars a year with his bad shoes, taste for cheap liquor, and his off the rack tweed jacket.

Actually, I was pretty impressed with the professor and so was Grady. He was calm, articulate and made several intellectual arguments that totally negated Stuart's point of view. After a couple minutes the teacher was toe-to-toe with Stuart and had him backed against the wall in a one-on-one conversation, with a finger in Stuart's chest. Hell, I was hoping to see the old man pop him in the mouth for being such an ass, but the exchange was only verbal. I was proud to see that a professor came to the rescue of the democratic process, as well as us Veterans. As it turns out, the teacher was once a former combat veteran in the Korean War and was in on the initial landing at Inchon in 1950.

As Stuart was getting an ear full, Grady and I left the party with a smile and went out front for a smoke. No sooner did I get outside I began shaking, not from the cold, but from having so much pent up anger and adrenaline that I could have beat Stuart back to his ancestors.

Grady apologized for bringing me in the middle and promised that if Stuart survived the night, he wouldn't be attending any gatherings in the future. Grady told me that Stuart was on unemployment twice that year, so he was one to talk. And over the last few months he'd been working odd jobs and was in the process of starting a multi-level marketing career to pay for the Cadillac he and his wife just bought. Grady said that Stuart was being supported by his wife and she was getting tired of his lazy ass. Grady said that Stuart was actually at the party to round up prospective clients for his new business venture.

As Grady tried to calm me down, he and I talked and laughed about the stupid look on Stuart's face, and about how proud we were of the professor. Then suddenly, the front door opened and out walked Stuart with his wife in tow. He quickly explained that he had to get home because his baby sitter wasn't allowed to stay too late. It was only seven-thirty. Grady and I knew Stuart was full of shit. He was just embarrassed and was looking for a quick exit before the professor broke a foot off in Stuart's ass. Grady shook his hand and thanked him for coming as I stood back hoping I didn't have to touch him.

Just as Grady and I were lighting our second cigarette, we heard Stuart yell out from across the street, "Dammit, a flat tire. Hey, you guys, I've got a good suit on here. Can you guys give me a hand with this tire?"

I never said a word. Grady was quick to respond. "No way, Stuart, we both have back problems, it would kill us to get down there. Sorry, pal, you're on your own."

Stuart pulled off his jacket, yanked out the spare tire, and changed the tire himself as he bitched at his wife to get in the car and to just shut the fuck up. Well, I guess things do work out for a reason, sometimes.

So you see, that's just a small example of the kind of shit I have to contend with. Most people like Stuart have broad statements and narrow minds, and veterans like Grady and me have to listen to their nonsense."

Smiling at me, Doctor Easton asked, "So, how did Stuart get the flat tire?"

Shrugging my shoulders, I answered, "No idea, the car looked perfectly fine when Grady and I were out there walking around it. But here is another example for you, doc.

A couple of weeks ago, around one in the afternoon, I

received a call from the school nurse that my daughter was ill and needed to be picked up. The nurse said that my daughter had an upset stomach and a temperature, and she thought it best for her to go home. My daughter's condition was nothing serious, but to me it was a fucking emergency. I tend to blow things out of proportion, especially when it concerns my little girl. By the way…she calls me papa.

After receiving the call, I jumped in my car and was on my way to pick her up because I didn't think it was a good idea for her to drive her vehicle, especially with a fever. About half way to the school a senior citizen in an old car the size of a boat pulled out in front of me. She was going twenty miles an hour in a forty-mile an hour zone, putting along at her own self-imposed speed limit. She could have waited until I passed because there was no one behind me for a mile, but no, she had to get in front of me when I was in the middle of an emergency.

I tried to pass but traffic was heavy in the other direction. I was so pissed that I started yelling and hitting the steering wheel of my car and screaming obscenities, which she could not hear. I was enraged. I drove two more miles with my anger raging before I reached the red light, where I was able to get around her.

When we reached the stoplight she pulled her car into the left turn lane and I pulled up beside her on the right, waiting for the light to change. I looked over at her, steaming with anger, but she continued to look straight ahead. Regardless, she prevented me from getting the green light and getting to my daughter, which I felt was detrimental to my mission.

I noticed her driver's side window was rolled about half way down. I sat there thinking how much pleasure it would give me to get out of the car, break the glass of her driver side window, grab her by the hair pull her head far enough through the window to slide her throat over the broken glass. I wanted to kill her in the most grotesque manner possible, then put her car in gear and send her ass out into oncoming traffic. How dare she stop me when my daughter is in need of her father? That old bitch had already lived her life. My daughter's life was just beginning. Fuck the old bitch!!

Of course, I never got out of my car and hurt the old woman, or made gestures she could see or shout obscenities she could hear. Actually, later in the day after I had my daughter safe at home and was sitting by the fireplace, I had time to think about how I acted, and you know what… fuck the old lady. I would have still had the same thoughts. I tried to feel some level of guilt for conjuring up such a scenario, especially about some old lady, but I couldn't. She was just an innocent bystander in the way of a Marine on a mission who was not about to take prisoners. I just thank my lucky stars I didn't have any weapons in the car."

Doctor Easton asked, "Jesus, what do you think brings these thoughts on? What's driving you to think like this?"

"You know, doc, people keep asking me that, and I haven't the faintest idea. My best guess would be that when I'm under stress, it causes my mind to shift into Marine mode, or what I call my evil other self, which guards the inner deep side of my thoughts, protecting itself and me from danger. Actually, I equate my thoughts and the two personalities to what I call my doppelganger. I guess to get into the various levels of my thoughts or evil side, it would be like trying to get into the White House by just knocking on the door. And there are several levels to getting into the one true evil dark side of my thinking. Sorry, that's my analogy anyway."

Dr. Easton leaned back in his seat and asked, "Can you tell me about getting into the mental White House. What's that all about, the different levels, I mean?"

Chapter Fourteen - Mental Politics

"Of course, this is only an analogy, but it's the best I can come up with. As far as I can tell there are several darker sides of my mind operating on various levels deep inside my head, and from day to day it's hard to tell which level I'm on. At least that is the way I see it.

To me, it seems the outer core of my mind deals with the unimportant day-to-day bullshit like keeping me safe or functioning normally at work. Whenever I'm confronted with stress I respond differently to situations without thinking as my mind is always on the alert switching from level to level to deal with any threat. From what I can tell, it tends to be the security forces within my mind trying to keep me safe. It's harder to access and I rarely see it, but believe me, it's there when I need it.

And finally, the deeper, darker side of my personality is untouchable deep inside my soul. The best I can tell, it's what's left over from my experiences and tour overseas. Whenever I have to access that part of my personality, I'm usually not a very pleasant person to be around. Deep inside me is some type of military demon, if you will, and if it's ever forced from its secure location, well, I'm not sure that we're in the right venue should that personality surface. It sure as shit never surfaced since I have become a civilian, and I am afraid that if it did, I could crack the earth in half right through the core."

Focused on what I said, Doctor Easton asked, "I'm curious…what would it take in order for you to go that deep, mentally? I mean would it be someone threatening your life, or maybe a death in the family or some horrible event like that? In other words, what could possibly trigger such anger inside of you?"

"Well, as I said, my best analogy is that it's like trying to get into the White House to see the President of the United States. I know it sounds silly, doc, but that's the way my mind works. So here goes. As you well know, it's not that easy to walk into the White House and demand to see the President. Of course, it is possible, but the question is, are any of you willing to make the trip, especially with security being so tight, and what is worse, if you don't have an appointment and try to force your way in?

When you first make the attempt you must get past the Secret Service and their security. It's important to know they respond to every situation like suspicious people at an unexpected knock at the door, the snapping of a twig or anyone or anything out of the ordinary that could be perceived as a threat. If they go into action, it's your ass. Their mission is to jealously protect the President, regardless of the situation. And you all know what the real Secret Service is capable of. They never fail. Well, except for that Kennedy thing, but we'll talk about that some other time.

If for some reason you successfully negotiate your way past the Secret Service, which I doubt you ever will, you then come face to face with the Chief of Staff. That man is second to the President. Him, you might actually like. The Chief of Staff is bright, personable, well educated, intelligent, rational, a clear thinker, and a difficult person to get around. And for the times when negotiations break down, he keeps the Secret Service very close at hand. The Chief of Staff's primary job is to assess the level of threat against the President and then hand the matter over to the Secret Service to neutralize.

But just for shits and giggles, let's say you are lucky enough to get past the Chief of Staff. You might be a genuine threat, or someone stupid enough to try to get between me and the safety of my children. It doesn't matter how you got past the Chief of Staff, you have just arrived in the war room, and the President is only interested in the safety and security of his family, putting himself second, and he jealously defends it all. At that point, it's your ass, I shit you not. If you live through it, I would be genuinely surprised."

I picked up my coffee cup and said, "What do you think?"

Closely scanning me with his eyes, Doctor Easton quietly asks, "Gary, who am I talking to right now?"

A little surprised, I answered, "Well, you're talking to me. It's kind of hard to explain. Here's a different analogy for you, doc. I would say that I am like a small boat tied to the dock in a raging storm. I always feel threatened by those I don't trust, and like the little boat, I don't have the strength to stay afloat against all the wind and big waves of the sea. The small boat is tossed and slammed up against the dock from all the outside forces, unable to fight the raging currents that are constantly pulling and pushing him in different directions.

Sometimes, it's like that side of me is being pulled in two directions, and I don't know which team to play for. Although I do feel safe the closer I get to the President, or what I call my deeper darker side. That's my comfort zone, and as the days pass, I get closer to the Oval Office, and farther from thinking and acting as a civilian. Actually, right now I think that I'm trapped between these two worlds and live in a constant state of confusion wanting to be loyal to the President, but not sure that I am. He has kept me alive this long, why should I begin to doubt him now?

The way I see my current mental state is that I can still communicate with the outside world, but most of the information I receive or communicate is distorted or fogged in, like it goes through a filter or some other translation. The security staff in my mind does not want me to lose that part of my attitude and personality, which once kept me safe and secure during all my dangerous times overseas.

Now, if you are asking if I want to be free of the chain of command and out of my mental politics, I'm not sure that I do. It's like me asking if there were a chance, could you do without your eyesight, or maybe one of your appendages? I guess you would learn to adjust but why do it if you don't have to?"

I pause for a sip of my cold coffee as Dr. Easton sits there in deep thought with his eyes fixed firmly upon me.

Doctor Easton asks, "I'm curious. How do you generally feel about the civilian sector? What if you found a job out here in the civilian sector that you actually like, would you have a sense of loyalty to that company like you did in the Marines?"

Chapter Fifteen - Workers Bill of Rights

I answer, "No, I don't think so, doc. There is no way I would ever be loyal to a corporation after they've accused me of being a threat to the workplace. When I began having troubles with my escalating PTSD, I went to the company for help. I didn't have a choice or any other place to turn for help, and I damn sure wasn't interested in losing my job.

I don't know if you are aware of it, but to prove to my managers that I had PTSD, I even turned over the most recent copy of my disability from the Veteran's Administration. The paperwork I gave them was very detailed, which also turned out to be a big fucking mistake on my part. I should have known better. My manager took that information and accused me of being a threat to the workplace. What kind of shit is that? They could see I needed help but all they could do was to look for a way to get me the fuck out of the company, and fast.

So, you ask about my loyalty to the company, well, what about their loyalty to their employees? No, I'm not loyal, not by a long shot. I can't believe how narrow-minded and two-faced people like that can be.

The managers were constantly telling their employees that we all must work as a team, pull together, look out for one another, and think of the company first. Well, that all works well when you're trying to motivate a room full of employees, but when it's one-on-one, their philosophy took on an entirely different face, especially when cost comes into play. You have to remember, out here in the civilian sector, it's all about money, not employees, or loyalty and dedication, just money. The company must move forward and the product must get out the door. It is all very conservative; it's cold, callous, and impersonal.

On one hand, they smile and tell me they're going to do everything in their power to help me, but in reality, they're secretly working in the shadows hatching some fucking scheme to force me out of the company. That's some teamwork, huh?

You want to know what fascinates me about American companies today? When you're hired, they ask for loyalty, dedication, to be a team player, and if you ever leave the company, they expect at least a two-week notice. But here's the interesting part. If a company has to start laying off employees due to piss-poor managers making piss-poor decisions, all we get is a tap on the shoulder and shown the door. Why isn't there a two-week notice for the employees when their shit hits the fan? Why is it always a one-way street with them? You want to know why, it's because they can get away with it, that's why. They don't want to give you a notice, fearing you will split from the company into the arms of a competitor, or that you may reformat all their hard drives or steal company secrets before you leave. They're just greedy, stupid and paranoid, and I fucking hate them, all of them. Here, let me give you an example of what I'm talking about. This really pisses me off, so bear with me.

I remember a few years back when a friend of mine in California worked for a different company than me, and after he received his degree at night school, he began looking for different work and more money. My friend put his resume out there with several different businesses looking for that bigger and better paycheck and luckily, after months of applying, got an interview with a company he seemed to like. Finally, after a third interview, he got an offer from the company. My buddy, being naive, accepted the position over the phone before getting the agreement down on paper. He was really excited about the new opportunity and so was his wife.

My friend told his new employer that he couldn't start for a couple of weeks because he wanted to do the right thing and give his current employer the customary two-week notice. The new employer had no problem with that, and told him to report for work in two weeks. And in the meantime they would get the paperwork in order in preparation for his arrival. The new company told him they would fax him over some information on benefits later in the day, if it would not be a problem with the company where he worked. My friend told his new boss to fax it over, no one would mind because the companies were not competitors.

My buddy, a good hard working husband and father, was very excited about his new position, and finally thought life was getting better for him and his family. With the new job he would be getting more money, better benefits, and he could finally tell his wife that she could quit working and stay home with their baby daughter. He was very excited about this new job and promotion.

After getting the good news, my buddy, who was a good honest Christian, went to his current boss that morning and informed him that he'd accepted a position with another company, but not a competitor, and he was officially giving his two-week notice. You want to how that stand-up, team-playing manager responded to the news?

His manager had my friend escorted out of the building fifteen minutes later, with the words, "I'm giving my two-week notice," still hanging in the air. His manager called Human Resources, asked for his log notes, security badge, and company credit card. They had security stand over him while he cleaned out his desk and a security guard escorted my friend out of the building, and all before nine o'clock in the morning. How's that for being a loyal team playing business manager?

The hard part of this story was when the new company that hired him called for my friend at work later that day to give him some benefits information on his new position. But since he did not answer, the call rolled over to an administrative assistant. The secretary, being the dumb shit she is, informed my friend's new employer that she had seen him escorted out of the building by security, and was told by the manager that he had been fired and was no longer with the company.

Well, my friend's new employer looked very unfavorably on their future employees being fired, so, they called him at home leaving a message on his machine that said that they had second thoughts on him working for their company, and that he was no longer considered for a position at their firm. My friend called them and tried to explain that it was all a big misunderstanding, that he was not fired, just asked to leave because he gave his notice, and that the administrative assistant was misinformed. Well, the manager at the company that hired him did not believe a word he said. He told my buddy that he already talked to the administrative assistant and she told him the truth. They refused to hire him and hung up.

And you want to know what happened next? Because of a slow economy, and being over qualified for every position he applied for, my friend could not find work for months. He had maxed out his credit cards and the only jobs that were available were fast food or retail department stores. And when he decided that some money was better than no money, he went to work. It wasn't for much more than minimum wage, and the hours he worked were not in alignment to what shift his wife was working. And you can't support a family on shit wages like that. He had to fill in the blanks of his monthly debt by maxing out his wife's credit cards. They even took out a small loan to help float them till things picked up. But they defaulted on the loan and were about to get their wages garnished and their cars repossessed. And all of this was in addition to the student loans he had taken out and became delinquent on. The shit was closing in on my buddy.

After a few months of trying to seek gainful employment and make ends meet, his loving, loyal, till death do us part wife, left his happy ass, taking the daughter, telling her husband that he needed to spend some time alone to get in touch with his feelings-the bitch.

The beautiful wife he once bragged so highly of left his young ass and she didn't care in the least. He never got her back, regardless of all his crying and begging. She remarried four months after leaving, and his daughter now calls someone else daddy.

So, you see. Regardless of what these people tell me, I will never trust a corporation. I will never be loyal to them, and I couldn't care less whether they succeed or fail. Every time the stock market takes a dip, or a corporation goes bankrupt, or a bank closes, believe me, it puts a smile on my face, especially if it's a fucking bank. Man, that's masturbating material right there when a bank goes under.

I love it when these team playing companies, as they like to call themselves, go under, because if they fail it's because they deserved to fail. You know the way I see it: a company can only be destroyed from within. If they fail, it's their own fault, so they deserve to go under. The only thing I would remotely feel bad about is the employees that get fucked along the way because of the company's piss-poor planning and shit-head managers that think they know everything. Fuck them, is all I say. Let them burn. And all this bullshit will continue until someone get the balls to issue an Employee's Bill of Rights.

To me, trying to survive in a corporation is like working in a Communist society. You follow orders because someone is always watching. Don't ever say anything against the company because someone is always listening. You must be politically correct because someone is always monitoring you, and you have to always be on the alert, never trusting anyone at anytime, because tomorrow, it could be your ass getting escorted out the door and home to a Gulag led wife.

But, hey, I'm not bitter. As far as I'm concerned, they can all go and fuck themselves. I have so much hate for these team players that if I ever do work for a corporation again, I will do everything in my power to create as much chaos and havoc as possible to destroy them from within.

You want to know why? Because I'm not there to be a team player, I'm only there for the money, not loyalty, not dedication, not believing in the fact that this company will really take us into the new twenty-first century. Most of these corporations out here today are a trade away from laying their workers off and the corporate officers escaping to some beach in Club-Med with the employee's retirement funds. Just wait, you'll see. They're not the Marine Corps, you know!"

I stop to catch my breath, and lean back to pick up my coffee cup. I see Dr. Easton taking notes. He then stopped, looked up and said, "You're right; I don't think you're bitter, just pissed. This is good information and I'm glad you brought it up. But I'm curious, what happened to your friend, the one whose wife left him. Did he eventually get a better job?"

"He killed himself. Well, by accident anyway. He was drinking and had taken some other pills, whatever. The combination, what I call a Hollywood cocktail, killed him. No one found him for a fucking week. Can you believe that shit?"

"Oh man. I'm so sorry. How long ago did this happen?

"I think five years or so, I forget. I have always believed his death had something to do with him not getting that new job, and then his wife leaving him and taking the baby. It's just a guess, but I'm pretty sure I'm right. You know, one thing led to another, and now he's dead, all because of a communication problem at his fucking job. I wish I knew who his fucking boss was that had him escorted out that morning. I'd shotgun that bastard."

With a sorrowful look on his face, Doctor Easton said, "Well, I'm sorry that happened to your friend. But now that we're talking about work, let's switch gears and have you tell me about the problems you've been having on the job. Just start from the beginning of your work issues, and then bring me up to speed on the problems that brought you here today. Whenever you're ready, this one I can't wait to hear!"

Chapter Sixteen - The Civilian Sector

Trying to think of where to begin, I said, "As a civilian working in a corporation, I'm nothing more than just another face in the crowd surrounded by a world of whining, politically correct, self-absorbed people trapped in their own individual greedy worlds wrapped in a blanket of their own inner turmoil. Basically, I'm in a living hell and there's no ladder to the top, especially for me, or people like me.

I think I hate people, doc. I get tired of listening to their shit or even being around them, for that matter. Did you know that since my discharge from the Marines, I've worked for fourteen different companies, and regardless of the job, I've always had troubles getting along with the people? It doesn't matter where I've worked or the position I held, it was always the same. The people irritate the shit out of me, and for some reason I get on their nerves as well...probably because they bore the hell out of me. I'm sick of listening to their shit, and I usually let them know it. What a bunch of fucking crybabies.

Every day it's the same shit. If they're not talking about their money problems, its trouble with their boss, trouble with another coworker, how much they hate their jobs, their cheating spouses, or how they are underpaid and over worked. I know the employees who are sleeping around at work, who's doing cocaine, the ones that are alcoholics, the gays, the lesbians, and of course, the employees who actually give a shit about the job. And the latter group I just mentioned is rare for sure, especially where I work! Doc, I don't think Americans like to work.

What's worse, gossip runs rampant in the private sector. The problem here is people feel they need to tell me about all the shit going on in their lives, and I don't want to hear any of it. I seem to always be within earshot of all of the gossip and I try to avoid it at all costs, but I'm not that lucky.

And of all the problems I've experienced since my discharge, the political correctness is enough to drive the sanest person into a straight jacket. It's nothing more than a few overweight ass-wipes who throw a wrench in the system and fuck it up for everyone else. Now I can handle just about anything but when I have to live and work around dip-shits like this, it's a wonder my cap didn't snap years ago. And hell, I'm not the only one.

First, let me step back a few months and bring you up to speed on how all this shit got started and it'll be a little clearer. For five years I worked for the same communications company. They're not a bad company I guess, up and coming with an IPO, and they seem to be generating new business. The company was started with three owners who began on a shoestring budget and now have grown the business into the beginnings of what might be a major corporation in a few years. My problem is not with the owners; hell, they're decent people. My problem is with the shit-heads way down the food chain in mid-management and lower.

In the beginning, I was hired as a problem solver in the company. The job I could handle, but I really didn't like the management staff above me. I found them all to be too lax, judgmental, and they had a grandfather clause for anyone who went to the same church as them. They had their favorites and I wasn't one of them. So, knowing that I had officially hit the glass ceiling for the anti-religious, I decided to look for work elsewhere in the company.

After a couple of weeks of searching, I found exactly what I was looking for. I applied and was hired to negotiate outside company contracts working with Japan, the Philippines, and several domestic companies out of California and Florida who were our outsourcers and field service teams. I figured the new position would keep me mentally stimulated, and give me a chance to start fresh with a new management staff.

As far as the new job was concerned, I enjoyed the work in the beginning. I had a nice office, great benefits, thirty days paid vacation, and a chance to travel overseas two or three times a year. The job became challenging, which I liked, but something happened to me. In the maze of hundreds of faces within my department, I noticed that I was just another name hanging on a cubicle wall. But due to my new humdrum career, something began to stir inside of me. I felt that I needed more, something to stimulate me. I was lacking something on my new job that I had on my old job- an identity.

In my old job I was at the top of my game. I was needed, I stayed busy, I was always on the go, and above all, if anyone had a problem with our communication equipment or were about to sue the company, management sent the problems to me- or me to the problem. I loved the recognition and the praise I got from my peers, and of course, our clients. Everyone knew my name and as far as I could tell, everyone in my old job except the religious management pricks seemed to like and respect me.

But after a few weeks on my new job, I realized that I didn't have the power, the budget, or influence my old position offered. Basically, I was now a worker bee sitting in a cubicle crunching numbers, and the walls were beginning to close in around me. Within my six by seven foot cell that I called my office, I'm wedged between a desk and chair, computer equipment, filing cabinet, a large worktable, two white boards, a maze of wires, and people sitting in cubicles on three sides of me. I was surrounded in a prison of computer equipment, florescent lights, Venetian blinds, and about 150 people within the department who were starting to get on my nerves. For someone who's claustrophobic, it's a wonder I've survived as long as I did.

As I said, at the beginning I liked the job. As the new guy, I got along with managers and co-workers, and what I enjoyed most about the job was that in the beginning it kept me busy. I wanted to do a good job, so I threw myself into my work. From eight in the morning to six at night, I was knee deep in negotiations or working with our outsourcers who installed and maintained our communications equipment.

I became so focused I not only completed my regular duties, I asked for additional responsibilities to keep me busy. You know the old expression, idle hands. When I completed a project, I went to my manger, Steve, for additional work.

My new boss, Steve, was a good guy. He became impressed with my performance, but when projects became scarce he told me to slow my pace, because there was a lot of work to go around. After hearing that, it made me even more anxious to push myself harder. I took the time between projects to learn new things in the company and focus on doing my job better than anyone had ever done it before.

I wanted to be irreplaceable and recognized by management as a true asset to the company instead of some fucking worker bee who was a clock-watcher. I couldn't believe my manager told me to slow my pace. I needed more mental stimulation. But secretly, my real objective was to work my way into corporate management and wedge myself close to the owners and make myself invaluable. That was my goal anyway. And the best way to reach management was to be a reliable, irreplaceable worker.

Hell, I was on fire. I needed stimulation and excitement, not stagnation. To me, the company was dragging their feet and needed to speed things up. In my opinion, I could have run the company. From what I could see, management was poor at making timely decisions that needed to be made. But they were acting like government officials as they held meetings everyday and still decisions were not made. But to me, no job appeared to be too hard, or no obstacle too big, and after awhile I had convinced myself that one day I would be sitting in the big chair, the head of the company, if not one of the co-owners.

So I figured that I would negotiate for a while and then make a move to stair step my way into a career in upper management, and then on to the big dog's chair, where the real power and decision making was done. I could fucking bring the company into the new 21st century, because I had no problem making decisions, I had experience and I wasn't afraid to make a tough decision. It wasn't like being a combat Marine. It's just business without getting shot at. So making decisions in the civilian sector wasn't difficult for me. The only thing you can kill out here is your career.

No, I need to be in charge, controlling, directing, and instructing others. For some reason I needed to keep moving as if something were chasing me. A slow snail pace was not the life for me. I need stimulation, you know, going down the hill with my hair on fire and loving every minute of it. But even though I was willing to go above and beyond the call of duty, my enthusiasm was not well received, especially from my co-workers. As I continued to stay busy and assist my boss with clearing up old problems, another situation arose. Others within the department, mainly my peers, didn't share my enthusiasm and work ethic.

Mostly, my co-workers wouldn't have much to do with me, especially when Steve took their long overdue projects from them and gave them to me. As far as I was concerned, my co-workers were in my way, and were not needed. Hell I was doing my job and theirs. After they lost several projects, the sniveling little bastards would brush by me like a stranger in the night, and when they had to communicate with me, it was mostly through lengthy e-mails, which I ignored and deleted. They didn't like me and that suited me just fine.

Where my peers were concerned, I didn't associate with any of them anyway, so personally, I couldn't have cared less what they complained about. But observing my coworkers I managed to see that none of them had any real goals to speak of. They put in their almost eight hours a day, tinkered from project to project, and chatted in the halls talking about sports, politics or religion never gaining much ground toward moving up in the company, or moving the company forward. When quitting time rolled around, they were the first ones out the door to go home or hit the local pub. In my opinion they were nothing but a bunch of clock-watchers getting a paycheck and slowing the progress of the company.

I often wondered how people could live like that. My mind didn't work that way. I wanted work, and the more the better. And when I was assigned a project, I did it fast, did it well, and was looking for the next challenge. I was on fire, and it kept me busy, kept me focused, although I'm sure there are people in my department that would disagree with my last statement. But Steve was impressed with me, and that was all that counted, until I ran into some trouble with my

PTSD."

Doctor Easton asked, "Since we are on the subject, when did you start having troubles in the company? What do you think set everything in motion?"

Chapter Seventeen - Trouble in Paradise

"Well, I think it was after hearing of the suicide of one of my team members from the Marines that might have set my mind adrift, or at least I think that was what started it. Not long after receiving the news, things began to change for me, especially my thought process. It was like a shadow of darkness somehow appeared which prevented me from having rational thoughts and functioning normally among the mainstream population.

When I stepped from reality to that parallel universe of my mind I became unpredictable, moody and sometimes dangerous. It forced my attitude to change from calm and reasonable to one of hate, distrust, and explosive outbursts toward anything or anyone that seemed to get in my way. I was left with nightmares, anxiety attacks and anger outbursts toward anyone who intruded on my personal space, which forced friends and co-workers to ostracize me. To me everything was becoming a threat, and I wasn't about to take prisoners.

Due to my mental confusion, I could not tolerate my co-workers, and at every turn I thought someone was out to sabotage my career or harm me in some way. I was a nervous wreck, everything frightened me, and I trusted no one. Every time a door slammed or a balloon popped I would suffer a panic attack. To me the old saying of 'business is war' took on a whole new meaning.

Daily, I sat at my desk sweating and shaking, my body reacting as if there were millions of pins trying to push out of my skin. I didn't know what was happening to me.

Suspicious of everything and everyone, the people around me began to get on my nerves more than ever, and I began to distrust them even more as the days passed. Whenever someone entered my cubicle, I would jump as if a grenade went off. I trusted no one, and at every turn I began to think people were watching me, monitoring me, looking over my shoulder.

A month later, I was a mess. I was only sleeping three hours a night, and at every turn, I thought my days were numbered at the company. I began thinking I was being set up for the kill, thinking the company wanted me gone. I knew every eye in the company was upon me, staring and whispering their venomous gossip.

My attitude began to get worse and my work faltered. Basically, I was doing the minimum, just like my peers, but to me, I was slipping fast. For some reason I kept thinking that I was about to lose my job, and I was worried as hell. I just knew that any day I would receive a tap on the shoulder and be asked into the security office and be released from the company. Then suddenly, something happened, something I could not explain, nothing mental, but physical."

Chapter Eighteen - Chest Pains

"A few days later, I was sitting at my desk staring at the walls, when I began to have chest pains, and they hurt. At first I just blew it off, but as the pain increased, a red flag surfaced. I became concerned. Not only was my chest and mid-section hurting; I had a pain running down my left arm, and a shortness of breath. My mid-section felt as if a belt were squeezing the air out of me.

Knowing something was definitely wrong; I panicked and immediately called my doctor. He told me to drop everything and go see the company nurse right away. He thought I might be having a heart attack. I told him that I didn't trust anyone at the company. I figured the company would let me die and no one at the company would give a fuck. So, I went to see him, because I was not about to die in that unpatriotic shit hole. Without giving it a second thought, I jumped into my car and rushed to the doctor.

My physician is Doctor Mark Tomlin, a former Navy Doctor turned civilian, but he misses the excitement and travel of the military. Dr. Tomlin is tall, and in good physical condition-a jogger and a vegetarian, I believe. He's been my doctor for a few years now, and we had an excellent rapport. On several occasions we discussed our experiences overseas, and from time to time we've played a little golf together. He's a good friend, and happens to be one of the few people I trust in life. He kept an eye on me.

After a series of tests, blood work, and an EKG, the good doctor found nothing wrong with my heart that he could see. He told me that I might be having a panic attack, which is sometimes called an anxiety attack. He said the symptoms sometimes mimic that of a heart attack but are rarely fatal;

they just make you think you're dying.

He told me that panic attacks usually come on when a person is under a lot of stress. Wonder where he got that idea? After my examination, he still questioned my condition, and the pain running down my arm, and thought it was better to be safe than sorry. He then referred me to the hospital for a stress test.

By three o'clock I had several electrodes covering my chest and was huffing and puffing on a treadmill, which hurt my back more than my heart. I figured if chest pains didn't kill me, the exhaustion of running in place would. Toward the end of the test, the cardiologist, an older, overweight, glib man, with a pack of Camel non-filtered cigarettes in his shirt pocket had me in a dead run on the machine at the maximum incline.

The doctor said jokingly, "Stop, stop, stop, you're going to break my machine. Hell, son, there is nothing wrong with your heart. You need to go back to your doctor and have him look for other ailments. You probably just have a turd cross ways in you. Get dressed; I'll have the results sent over to your doctor. He'll want to see you again, I'm sure." I got dressed and drove straight home.

By four o'clock I was lying on the couch thinking about my troubles and trying to work through an anxiety attack. The thought of going back to work sent a chill through my body, but a thought did occur to me. Maybe if I ask the company for help, I would be able to keep my job and probably get a few days off to recuperate. That had to be the right thing to do. If I tell management about my troubles, they are sure to help me, especially my immediate manager, Steve.

Of all the thoughts that were running through my head, that idea seemed to be the most logical. I thought, if I go to management and lay it all out on the table about my stress and PTSD, they would come to my rescue. My reasoning was that I had nothing to lose.

Still fearing that I was about to lose my job, I purposely missed the next two days of work, trying everything from alcohol to pain killers to suppress my anxiety and depression. I knew my mental health was getting worse, and my sixteen-year-old daughter could see it. Casi was concerned, but kept it to herself.

With my depression at an all time low, and panic attacks at three a day, I spent most of my free time alone. Every night, sleep ended with a nightmare and my days were mostly spent consuming booze to kill the memory of the previous night's nightmare.

That weekend I popped prescription pain pills and slept only two to three hours a night. During the day I was consumed with depression, confusion, and a lot of horrible thoughts. What will happen to me at work? If I lose my job, how will I support my daughter? What happens if I die tomorrow?

I thought to my self- at my age and a poor attitude to boot, I'm not exactly the most marketable shark in the sea. I'm too old and wrapped too tight to begin looking for a new career again, or starting some entry-level position standing in line behind guys half my age and better educated. There's not a very big demand for a burned-out combat Marine with Post Traumatic Stress Disorder on his record. So when Sunday night rolled around, I didn't sleep a wink."

Chapter Nineteen - Monday Morning

"The following Monday morning I went back to work. I couldn't go in with alcohol on my breath, and if I did, someone would detect it, and run like a sissy to tell the boss, trying to get me fired. So, to play it safe, I decided to pop pain pills during the day to help relieve some of my anxieties. I took three Percocet every four hours, which helped a little. The only problem with that drug is that it's really addictive and hard to get. The pills kept my attitude and personality in check, but down deep I still had a problem.

At work I stayed within my small cubicle and pretended to look busy, but in truth, I was stoned and worried about my future. Regardless of how much I drank or how many pills I popped, my depression and anxieties were still there. Just to compound the problem, I still had the negative thoughts about losing my job, which continued to play hell on my nerves. Why I thought that way, I have no idea. I had to do something; I felt the axe would be dropped on my career at any day, and I was determined to salvage what was left of an eighty-thousand-dollar a year income.

Overall, I was a mess. It was no longer possible for me to do my job without using some type of suppressant as a crutch to kill anxiety or the negative thoughts running through my head. I had nowhere to turn and no one to talk to. I couldn't go back to my doctor looking for more pain pills, and I wasn't about to go into the VA and lay it all out. I didn't want to talk to anyone. I wanted to be alone, but I had to be at work if I wanted a paycheck.

As far as I was concerned, I had talked myself into asking for help, and why not? The company would not fire someone who came to them first. It wouldn't be right. Something like that would put the company in a precarious legal position. I knew they would understand my problem and give me help me if I asked. But the trick was to get to them first, before they got to me. I also had to be careful who I asked for help, and how I went about it.

The next day, Tuesday, I managed to catch my supervisor alone and approached him. I said, "Hey, Steve, you have a minute to talk?" He stopped checking his E-mail and turned to me.

He said, "Yeah, I have time, what's on your mind, let's sit over here?" He and I stepped around the corner to one of the small conference rooms. Steve sat down, leaned back with a pen and paper in hand, and I sat in a chair opposite him.

"Steve, if possible, and if you have the time, I would like for you to set up a meeting for me tomorrow. I would like to meet with you and our Department manager as soon as possible about something very personal."

The look on Steve's face went from a half smile to a relaxed position as he sat up straight rubbing both his hands on the edge of the table. Steve was suspicious at my request. I could imagine the thoughts that must have been running through his head. What could this guy possibly need that would require our department manager's involvement? Besides, our department manager was a dickhead and Steve didn't like talking to him if there was no need.

He said, "Sure, I can try for tomorrow, but as you know, we're pretty busy right now with the end of the quarter and all. But if it's that important to you, I think we can manage something. Is there anything I can do in the mean time to help you?"

I replied, "No, I'd rather not. It's personal and I need all the input I can get. So, if you don't mind, I'd prefer to wait until tomorrow. I'd greatly appreciate it."

Still concerned about my request, my supervisor said, "I'll tell you what I'll do. I've got a meeting in a couple hours with Michael, so I will bring up your request at the end of our meeting, and see what we can put together. Now, I can't promise tomorrow, but I'll try. Will that work?" He then stood.

I stood up and said, "Steve, I would appreciate anything you can do for me. Thanks." We then shook hands, and I went back to my desk. I sat down, noticing my breathing was shallow and rapid, and I began to sweat profusely. I had just opened the door, and God only know what would be released. But I had confidence in Steve, but no one else in the company.

Later that same day, I was a little more relaxed when Steve approached my cubicle. He walked in and sat down, still sporting a confused look about what was so personal to me that it would require two managers. He said, "I talked to Michael about your request, and he agreed to a meeting tomorrow for the three of us at ten o'clock in the cafeteria. Will that work?"

"Yeah, that will work great, Steve, I'll be there. I really appreciate you getting this set up on such short notice. Thanks again."

He said, "Not a problem. In the mean time, if there is anything I can do, just let me know." He then stood. He looked as if he wanted to ask me a question, but hesitated. He then walked out. I was glad he didn't attempt to quiz me about the nature of the meeting. I might have given in and told him everything, but I don't think I could have stomached the embarrassment of explaining my problems twice. Besides, I brought him in on this as a courtesy; it's the department manager that has the power to make the necessary decisions concerning my problem.

Later that night my worries continued. I worried about how I'd introduce my problem to the two managers and the sensitive VA paperwork I would be putting in their hands that exposed everything about my condition. One thing was for sure; I wasn't about to mention a word about the death of my friend, and how that might have set my PTSD into full swing. No, I figured it would be best to just keep my mouth shut about why I had a problem."

Doctor Easton then spoke up, "Gary, what made you feel you were about to be fired? Did someone at the company give you some indication that they were unhappy with your work, or approach you in some way?" I was hoping to go the entire day without that question.

"No, nothing like that," I said. "For some reason I was under the impression that my job was on the line and everyone was out to get me. I can't explain it, but I was worried. Now in retrospect, I would have to say it must have been my Post Traumatic Stress Disorder, but I can't be sure. Actually, I was about to get to that, buddy."

Doctor Easton said, "Okay, no worries." He then went back to writing on his legal pad. I continued.

Chapter Twenty - Meeting Management

"On the day of the meeting, Michael, Steve and I met in the company's cafeteria at ten o'clock sharp. As we set at the table with our coffee in hand, I noticed the two of them appeared to be wondering as to why I needed a personal session with two managers. The department manager knew nothing more than we were scheduled to meet, and my supervisor, Steve, looked a little worried that I may have called the meeting to rat him out about problems within the department.

My immediate supervisor had nothing to worry about. Steve might be a little narcissistic, but he never approached me to discuss problems about my work performance. As far as I could tell, he never thought my job to be in jeopardy. It was me that had the problem, but at the time, I was paranoid, thinking the company was out to get me. Who knows, if I had just kept my mouth shut and moved on with my life, maybe none of this shit would have ever happened.

Now, as far as my department head, Michael, he is a typical bottom line manager who puts in more than his fair share of overtime to achieve company objectives. He is a short, older man in his mid-fifties with a PhD in whatever, who appeared to be very bright, personable, and focused on the job, when you could get him to talk with you. I could tell he didn't like people, and it showed.

If someone walked up to Michael, it had better be about something job related. He had no time for people or idle bullshit, and that is why I respected him. I've never had much contact with him unless we were in a company meeting, and even then, it was just for updates on current projects. His responsibility was to keep the department moving and his managers on the ball, and from what I could tell, he was doing a fine job of keeping the company in the black. On my report card he gets an "A" on the job but an "F" dealing with people. Hell, he even ate lunch alone in the cafeteria as he read reports.

When the meeting started, I held nothing back. I put my problems on the table. I explained to the managers how the VA diagnosed me with a condition called Post Traumatic Stress Disorder, which is a disease that affects trauma victims. I then described my current problems at work and the stress I was under, making it difficult for me to meet my objectives. My reasoning for the flare up was that I had been trying to do too much, too fast and it caught up with me. Then I gave them my most recent paperwork from the Veterans Administration, which described, in detail, my current mental condition and all about my PTSD. The VA paperwork I handed over was quite explicit. A novice reading it would quickly form a negative opinion and probably distrust me from that moment on. But the two managers were professionals and I was expecting their help and their trust to get me on the right track.

But I wasn't concerned about what they thought of me. I wanted their help. I knew these men had no experience in dealing with veterans and PTSD; their job was to negotiate and bring in big bucks for the company. But they did have the one thing I didn't. They had the power to put the wheels in motion to get me the help and the time off that I needed to recover.

In the process of explaining my mental instability, I even offered the managers examples of the trauma I experienced overseas: my jungle experiences, some of the interrogations we did, the helicopter crash, and the affect it had on me.

But I never mentioned the incident about the baby."

Fuck, fuck, and fuck some more. What in the hell possessed me to bring that fucking shit up about the baby I will never know. I hoped Dr. Easton would just let it pass. I saw Dr. Easton draw his eyebrows together but said nothing. He's smart and I doubt he'll forget it.

After my slight mental drift, I continued with my story. "During my long explanation of my current mental issues, both the managers listened attentively trying to piece all this information together, but I could tell from their reactions that my information was way out of their depth. This was a lot of information for them to take in, and I could see it on their faces. But they acted concerned, hopefully giving me the benefit of the doubt.

As I continued to explain my condition, the two of them passed the VA paperwork between them, and took notes. After concluding, my manager spoke up to say that they were surprised to hear that I had such a condition, and the reason why I wanted this meeting caught them completely by surprise. And that surprised me. I think my supervisor, Steve, rested a little easier knowing the meeting wasn't about his management abilities. After he heard what I had to say he looked a little more chipper that when he first sat down. He had no reason to worry. He was a good guy, and I had a good feeling that regardless of what he read in my VA paperwork, Steve would act in my best interest.

After I finished with my PTSD experiences, I stopped talking, wanting to see how they reacted to what they were just told. The managers' first reaction was that of a relaxed and concerned nature as they asked me a few closing questions, writing down my answers."

Doctor Easton asked, "What kind of questions did they

ask you?"

"Well, you know the typical sort of questions a civilian would ask. What branch of the military was I in, where did I serve and when and if I ever killed anyone. Wow! That question caught me by surprise."

Without looking up, Doctor Easton asked, "How did you answer that?"

I said, "All I told them was, "Hey, ain't war hell?" That was the end of their questions."

Doctor Easton chuckled and said, "Way to go."

I continued. "When they were finished writing, Michael stood up beside the table and said, "Gary, you made the right decision by coming to us. I can assure you we will do everything in our power to help with whatever you need to get back on track. In the meantime, if there's anything you need I want you to see Steve and the two of us will get together and try to come up with a solution for you. In the meantime, I don't want you talking to anyone about what has transpired here today. You won't be doing yourself any favors if everybody in the department knows what's going on in your head. We have all the information we need, so let Steve and I work on this. Okay?" Steve then stood as well.

When a manager has had enough of your shit, they say, "Okay" and then stand to let you know they are ready to move on, that you are boring them. Michael then said, "Now, it may take a little while to get everything into play, so I just ask for your patience. And in the meantime if you need anything, see Steve here." I agreed and accepted, but suddenly Michael's reactions and mannerisms did not seem sincere to me. Something seemed different. At that point I wasn't sure if I trusted him, especially with my VA paperwork. Because of his expression, I wasn't convinced by his words of comfort, and feared that my job might still on the table. All of a sudden, it occurred to me that consulting my managers was not the right decision.

Needing to bring the meeting to a close, Michael looked at his watch and then glanced over at Steve and said, "You and I have another meeting to attend." As Michael turned to Steve, I noticed that he still had my VA paperwork and was placing it inside his large day timer. My intentions were for Michael and Steve to look over the material during the meeting and comment on it, but to give it back. I really didn't want the VA information leaving my side.

Michael held up my paperwork and said, "Gary, I need to have a further look at this, I hope you don't mind. I'll return it as soon as I'm finished, if that's all right?"

What the hell was I going to say, "No, that's mine, give it back?" Of course, I didn't say that, so I agreed, with a smile. What could I do? I'm the one that opened that door.

Then both Mike and Steve shook my hand and told me to hang in there, that we would be talking soon. I nodded with a smile. They both then turned and walked toward the coffee machine while talking quietly. I would have loved to know what they were talking about. With the way my mind was working, I kept thinking they were hatching some scheme to fire me anyway."

Doctor Easton asked, "Gary, I'm not saying that what you did with the paperwork was wrong, but if you were having these kinds of problems, why didn't you come to see me? I could have helped you with the anxieties and prescribed the right medications, I was only a phone call away. And when you were too ill to return to the company, I could have contacted your work and had something put in place out on your behalf. There are always other possibilities; you didn't have to go it alone. I wish you would have come to me."

"Yeah, me too, doc. With a million thoughts running through my head all day, my thinking was muddy and my mind was responding like a hundred movies at once were showing on one screen. I was lucky to even have the capacity to ask the company for help. But now that you mention it, you're right; I should have come here first, sorry. I just thought I needed to get my PTSD information to the managers before they got to me, if you know what I mean?" Looking over at Doctor Easton I noticed that he was taking notes and nodding, agreeing with me.

Doctor Easton asked, "What happened next? I can only imagine this story getting worse by the minute."

Chapter Twenty-One - Hurry up and Wait

Setting my coffee down I said, "You're right about that, doc. Well, I kept a low profile, you know. I was flying under the radar so to speak. I did my best to avoid contact with anyone in the department, and it worked for the most part. Two days after our meeting, my department manager, Michael, walked into my cubicle and asked me to meet him in his office. As I followed him, I kept trying to convince myself that I had made the right decision by entrusting management with such a critical piece of my personal history, and that they would take immediate action on my problem and see it through to the end.

Walking into Michael's office, I sat in the chair in front of his desk, and he took his seat. Before he even said a word, he slid my VA paperwork across the desk, where it dropped from the top of the desk onto my lap. I looked up with a curious look. From the way he acted, I thought for sure that he was going to tell me that I was fucked, and there was nothing the company could do to help me, and by the way, you're fired. But he didn't say that.

Avoiding eye contact with me, he said, "Gary, I called you in here to give you back the paperwork and inform you that Steve and I discussed your problem and came to a conclusion. To be honest with you, this problem is over our heads and out of our depth. So, we decided the best course of action would be to seek advice through other channels within the company that are better trained and equipped to handle this sort of situation."

I quickly replied in a not so confident voice. "You mean, Human Resources, right?" Shit, the Gestapo knows what's going on in my head. Now it was time to worry.

Michael looked up as if he were surprised that I already knew the answer. Jesus, I wasn't stupid, I have three degrees and know how to think. If he weren't able to help me, where else would he take my problem- Accounting? Michael and Steve asked me not to mention this to anyone, but they'd take my problem and my paperwork to the fucking Gestapo without consulting me first."

Doctor Easton asked, "How'd you feel about that?"

"Well, the damage had already been done, so what was I to do? Now all that was left was to hear him out.

Michael continued. "So, after careful consideration, Steve and I both agreed that the best thing to do in this situation was to consult Human Resources. HR has several people on staff that have years of experience in dealing with situations such as this. After Steve and I consulted with HR, their solution was to bring in someone from the outside, a professional psychologist to help you deal with the day-to-day stress of the job, and to work with you on the trouble you're having being around people. This morning the Human Resources manager contacted a local psychologist named Rupert Gray, and he agreed to meet with you. But in the meantime, we all think it best that you not take on any new projects at this time, and take it easy for awhile."

Feeling confident, Michael reclined in his chair and continued. "After HR contacted Mr. Gray, he suggested you take a break anytime you need it, and he will be in touch with you in a few days. Steve gave him your work phone number here at the company. Now, in the meantime, if work gets to be too much for you, we can even arrange for you to take time off without it affecting your available vacation time. All you have to do is let Steve know, and he'll see to it that you get the time you need in order to get through this.

We all just want you to know that we are here to help you, and you can trust us." Michael then smiled at me, but his eyes didn't smile. They remained stoic and cold.

I was cornered. There wasn't much else to say, so I just nodded appreciatively and thanked him for going the extra mile for me. I wasn't about to get into a pissing contest right there about him taking my problem to HR. Hey, I didn't have that kind of power, or patience.

After getting the information on the psychologist, I again thanked Michael for the help and walked out of his office. On my way out he gave me a pat on the back and said, "Don't you worry about a thing, Gary, we're on top of this."

I went back to my office and as usual, I had something to worry about. As you can see, doc, Rupert Gray was nowhere to be found. Actually, I thought he was a figment of HR's imagination. The guy never called me, and when I called the number they gave me, the number was disconnected. Now, what kind of shit is that? To be honest, I didn't think the fucking guy ever existed until I got a call from him yesterday.

And to make matters worse, I noticed the VA paperwork I'd given to Michael had the original staple removed in the upper left corner and then re-stapled. They made copies, doc, and figured I wouldn't notice.

In all honesty, I think they were trying, especially Steve. I was grateful for the help, but I was not thrilled at having Human Resources in my corner. Earlier when I said, "Gestapo," I wasn't bullshitting. I don't know whether you've ever had any experience with these fucking people or not, but they are the worst sort of people to have in your corner. First off, they root for the company one hundred percent, without question and no exceptions. If you have a beef with the company, they stand firm without any flexibility whatsoever, and God forbid should you ever have a comment about company policy. And if there's ever a problem and your name comes up, well, your happy ass is on their short list when layoffs come around, or you're fired for whatever trumped-up reason they can muster from their feeble minds and coffee stained teeth.

So, as you can see, I was not elated to have HR rooting in my corner. Anyway, the damage had been done. Whether I liked it or not, HR and management would be working on a way to help me out, and that scared me the most.

Even though I hated human resources more than you can imagine, there was still another problem in the company that stressed me out. I still had to work with four of the worst crybabies, kiss ass peers in my department who were always getting on my nerves or involving themselves in things that were none of their business."

Doctor Easton spoke up and asked, "Yeah, let's go there for a minute, give me some examples of your co-workers behavior."

Chapter Twenty-Two - The Slackers

"Okay, here are some examples for you, doc. One afternoon, I was on my way to meet with upper management to show some overhead slides concerning recent negotiations. I was running late when I turned from the hallway to pass between the worker cubicles as a short cut to my meeting. I only got about ten feet before I came to a stop. There, before me, stood two women that worked in my department, named Anne and Grace. They were our fact checker paper pushers. They were standing in the aisle talking about something not company related, and when I walked upon them wanting to get by, Anne said in an angry voice, "We're busy, go around, asshole."

Already running late for my meeting, and a little pissed at Anne's comment, I immediately snapped and said in a loud voice, "Bullshit, get the FUCK out of the way. If you two can't find something productive to do, I'm sure that I can convince Steve to provide you with loads of work to keep your asses out of the aisles."

Needless to say they each took a step back and let me pass. As I walked by, I heard Grace say in a low voice, "Fucking asshole, who does he think he is-upper management?"

You see this is the kind of shit I have to contend with everyday. These two fat bitches sit around and do in a month what I can get done in a day. And in every department meeting when issues or problems are brought concerning issues in their work, they get loud and point the finger at other people in the department. They are always making excuses and are the first to blame someone instead of accepting responsibility for their own fuck ups.

For the life of me I can't see why the company keeps them

employed. Either Grace or Anne will miss every other Monday, giving the same old excuse that their kids are sick or they need a mental day off. And if a holiday comes up, you can bet your ass both of them will call in sick the day before the holiday starts, and the day after the holiday is over. No wonder women only get paid a portion of what a man makes. It's because of women like Grace and Anne.

Now, everyone knows that Grace is a drunk. She comes in reeking of alcohol as it seeps through her pores, and looking like she only had two hours of sleep. Hell, I only get four hours a night, and I don't have bags under my eyes or fall asleep at my desk.

And another thing, no one in our department could tell you the last time this woman took a bath. Instead of taking a shower, she smothers her fat ass in perfume, thinking no one will notice. God forbid I should have to sit next to her in a team meeting. I get nauseated just thinking about the bitch.

Her other half, Anne, is about fifty but not a drunk. She is just two hundred pounds overweight, has a bad attitude, and is lazy as hell. When she comes to work in the morning it takes her thirty minutes to just get up and running, all while bitching and moaning about having to be at work so early-at eight o'clock. But when four o'clock rolls around, she is waddling out the door so fast; her fat ass looks like two bulldogs trying to fight their way out of a sleeping bag. She is funny as hell to look at, but dumber than shit to talk to. Everyday you can hear her talking about her weight, and how she can't drop pounds because of a gland problem. Gland problem my ass, her problem is on the end of her fork.

You want to know what the most disgusting thing is

about her? She wears these tight spandex pants that show every ripple and dimple on her ass and thighs. She must think that people find her sexy since everyone is always looking at her. And lucky me, I can't go a day without her coming over to my cubicle to bitch about something. I can't stand it when she gets near me. Her fucking breath smells like decomposition, and her body odor smells like feet and armpits. So, on any day, Grace and Anne can be seen talking and bitching about the company, and how if they were running things, the company would be in better shape.

So as to not just pick on women here, the men in my department are even worse. First, there is Rafe, or Rafael or some shit, and in my opinion whoever named this fucker needs their ass whipped. This guy is forty years old and still lives with his mother. How he's lived this long without someone fucking killing him amazes me. He's one of the biggest kiss asses I have ever come across in my life. He would rat on his own mother if he thought it would score him some points with Steve. God forbid should anyone roll into work five minutes late. If you are late, you can bet your ass Rafe's writing it down in his personal notebook, or over at Steve's desk, whispering in his ear. He never went to Steve about me being late because I get in to work about thirty minutes before him.

Our supervisor, Steve, just humors him by rolling his eyes and telling him, "Rafe, it's noted, thanks." Rafe, the little prick, stands four foot nine inches and has a grudge against anyone an inch taller than him. He has short, thinning hair, which stands straight up, and he is always stroking his skimpy ass mustache while looking around the room for a conversation that might have started without him- the fucking little troll.

For some reason, he feels that he has to be in on every conversation in the department that's not business related. Personally, I think he feels that people on our team don't think he's smart. He is always bringing up facts around Steve or myself, trying to impress us with some obscure piece of information he picked up on the History Channel. And people think I'm nuts- fucking civilians.

The second of our six-person team is Gus, short for Gustov, the Christian fuck. This guy walks around the department irritating the shit out of me, quoting scripture about God did this, and Jesus did that, or the Lord works in mysterious ways, or it's God's will. I'm so fucking sick of hearing his shit; I'd like to stick a crucifix up his ass.

In addition to his annoying religious crap, I have never seen anyone who moves as slow as this fucker does. It's like he's moving in reverse. It's no wonder that Steve took projects from him and turned them over to me. If Gus gets an assignment, he first questions you into the void trying to understand the project, when all he had to do was read the fucking e-mail Steve sent him. And if the project required any thinking, Gus will then try to find a way to pawn the project off on someone else. I really feel sorry for Steve sometimes that he is not allowed to carry a gun at work.

Then, once Gus gets his project, it takes him weeks or even months to report back on something I could do in a day or two. Every Friday at our team meeting, Steve will ask, "Hey, Gus, what's the status on your project?"

Steve always gets the same answer, "It's nearly there, Steve. Jesus and I have just about got it licked, praise the Lord!"

Steve looks over at the rest of us and rolls his eyes. Personally, I would fire that incompetent lazy bastard and shove his fucking Bible so far up his ass it would tickle his ear. Goddamn, I hate that fucker. What I would like to do is tie that bastard to a chair in the storeroom, and staple his fucking eyelids open and make him watch as I rip his Bible apart one page at a time. I'm sure you know what I'm talking about?

Being around these people is like being stuck in a perpetual Wizard of Oz. Work is so bizarre, it's a miracle that anything gets done at all. No wonder Steve hired me. If I want to have an intelligent conversation I have to talk to Steve, or have a chat with my buddy, Aaron. Aaron tries to avoid my area all together. The reason is that Anne is sweet on him, and that scares Aaron. And I think Anne's big enough to take him down.

Anyway, while waiting on the help the company had promised, I happened to notice that two weeks had already passed, and not a word or an e-mail had come my way, and we were closing in on the Christmas break that would last two weeks. I was hoping they would get to me before we broke for the holiday. Not only had the company not kept me up to speed on what was happening, I still hadn't heard shit from the psychologist the company promised. I was told that he was the best. Yeah, he's the best at avoiding his clients by not having a phone, assuming he ever existed. But the phantom psychiatrist was the least of my problems.

So, I thought I would give Michael a visit to try and get an update on the status of my request and the help they offered. When I reached Michael's cubicle, he had not yet arrived at work. I pulled out a pen and leaned over his desk to leave him a note, but something caught my eye. I spotted my name at the top of some correspondence on his desk. Without fear of being caught I walked around his desk. There in plain view were stacks of e-mail's with my name highlighted at the top. I looked up and saw no one in the area; actually I was the first one in that morning. I wanted to have a better look at the paperwork. So, instead of reading it and getting caught, I rolled it up and put it in my briefcase.

I knew full well that if I were caught at Michael's desk or with the sensitive company information I would be fired on the spot. So, instead of keeping it at my desk I went down the corridor toward Aaron's desk. I would have him put the paperwork in his car and I would pick it up later that night at his house.

As I made my way down the corridor with my briefcase in hand, I spotted Michael coming toward me, but I kept walking as if I had never stole sensitive information off his desk. Michael asked, "You just get here?" That question caught me off guard. I guess the fact that he even spoke to me surprised me.

When I passed him I casually replied, "Yeah, but I need to grab a bite at the cafeteria before I get started, my daughter got off to a late start this morning, you know, teenagers."

As Michael passed me he nodded and smiled when he said, "Yeah, I've got three kids, I know how that is." What I wanted to do was knock his ass out with my briefcase, but they were only thoughts. I kept walking. For some reason, I had it in my mind that he was in on the conspiracy.

I made it to Aaron's desk without a problem, and when I explained the situation to him, he took the paperwork, placed it in his day planner, and stashed it safely in his girlfriend's car (she also worked for the company.) He told me to meet him at his house after work and we could go over the information together, which we did.

Later that evening while Aaron's girlfriend was brewing

up some coffee, Aaron and I read the e-mails, which caused a chill to run through my body. Somebody, and I suspect human resources, were obviously trying to build a case on me. The company was monitoring me. There had to be over a hundred of my e-mails and close to a hundred of my phone calls logged on more than fifty pages and neatly placed in a report for Michael's viewing.   All the information we were reviewing was not incriminating in any way and it was all company business. But doc, if you know Human Resources, they have the ability to turn chicken salad into chicken shit.

Besides the e-mails and phone calls, there were three pages in the back of the report that were devoted to nothing but my regular daily activities. Someone, probably fucking Rafe, that Communist tattletale, had logged when I arrived at work, when I left for lunch, when I returned from lunch, and when I left for the day. Someone was watching me. But who was watching me? My mind was definitely in high gear trying to figure that shit out. To me it was like being in the crosshairs of a sniper.

Aaron made an interesting observation, "Gary, if there is someone monitoring your every move, do you think it's possible they saw you take the report off of Michael's desk?"

He had a point, but I wasn't worried. Shit, the people in my department weren't that dedicated. I knew I was the only one in early that morning, and if someone did see me, they would need to be better at stealth than me, and where civilians are concerned, they're not that clever. And as far as the paperwork I took off Michael's desk, he'd never miss it. He's always misplacing shit and having people make him another copy.

It's easy to monitor me when there are a hundred people around, which makes it difficult for me to determine who the vermin could be. But once I discovered that I was being watched, I was constantly on the alert after that, but cautious not to let the asshole know that I know, you know?"

Doctor Easton said jokingly, "I know."

"From that moment on, I became suspicious of the ones who promised me help. And I knew that Human Resources had been rummaging through my desk, pulled my e-mails, and monitored my phone calls trying to find something they could use to build a case on me. I told you these bastards were evil. They are the only ones with that kind of power in the company. Just let me say this, if they were not behind it, they authorized it.

If the company was there to help me as they promised, they sure had a funny way of showing it. From what I could tell, I was under constant surveillance. But after a lengthy conversation with Aaron, we came to the conclusion that the best thing to do was to be on the watch, and to wait out the company to see what their next move might be. So, I waited for the company to make the next move."

Dr. Easton scratched his head and said, "I think you're right. It sounds to me like they wanted to know your every move to keep a close eye on you. So, when did they finally contact you about the help they promised?"

Chapter Twenty-Three - The Gestapo

I answered, "Worried about what could be taking so long, I thought of approaching management to see what the delay was, but in the end, I just decided they had all the information they needed, and it was their move. I wanted to see if they were sincere about the help they offered, or if their comments were nothing more than empty promises.

It was nearly a month since I first informed management of my problem, and I had all but given up on the company. Then, early one afternoon I was sitting at my desk waiting for an important teleconference call to begin when Michael, the department manager, walked into my office and asked if he could have a word with me. He then turned and walked out with a preoccupied look on his face.

As I followed him I kept thinking to myself that it was about time, I was finally going to get the help they promised. Walking behind Michael and trying to keep up with him, I wondered where he was taking me. I followed him into another area of the building and into a conference room that is normally used for visitors or security personnel. When Michael held the door open for me, I was surprised to see two other people in the room waiting for us. When I entered, they stood. Oh, what a brief meeting this was going to be.

Once I walked into the room, Michael introduced me to the Human Resources manager and to the company's security manager. The HR manager was a heavyset man about six feet tall. He was bald with a beard and small round glasses that he kept pushing up on his nose. But the most annoying thing about him was that he had pursed lips. When you looked at him, it looked like he wanted to give you a kiss or something. I had noticed him around the department from time to time, and heard he loved to fire people. Finally, I was face to face with the enemy. To be honest, I felt more like a prisoner of war about to be interrogated by some asshole that wanted to slip me the tongue.

Sitting across from the HR manager was the security manager. He looked to be in his late sixties and about six foot five with a rugged, wrinkled face, which had obviously been tarnished from years of sucking on bottle after bottle of vodka and pack after pack of cigarettes. He kept quiet for the entire meeting, but just the thought of him being in the same room with the three of us was enough to arouse my suspicions, and make me want a cigarette. Upon introductions I kept wondering why the security manager needed to be at this meeting with us. That question would soon be answered.

Michael spoke first by saying, "Gary, I will turn this meeting over to the HR manager, if you don't mind. He has a few things he wants to discuss with you." During his brief statement, he couldn't even look me in the eye. When I looked at him, he'd look away as if intimidated, or scared. Regardless, I know somewhere deep inside of him he knew Human Resources was setting me up to be fired, and Michael was uncomfortable with it. Anyway, the shit pot was about to be stirred and they all were going to make me lick the spoon.

The HR manager wasted no time as he said curtly, "Gary, it's been brought to our attention that your conduct in the company has been less than desirable, unprofessional if you will. The reason for this meeting is to inform you that we are sending you home for an unspecified time, without pay, pending an investigation due to your attitude toward your supervisor, Steve."

Well, that caught me completely by surprise. Not only was I not about to receive any help, I was being accused of having some sort of attitude toward Steve, one of the only guys in the building I actually liked, and trusted. As if I didn't have enough to worry about, now they lay this shit on me. Didn't I tell you HR was the fucking enemy? What a fucking cock-sucking ass-wipe this prick was.

I had a thousand thoughts running through my head, mostly about murder, dismemberment, and where to hide the bodies. At first I thought this was some kind of joke, but to look at any of them I could see they were all dead serious, especially that fat HR manager piece of shit. Suddenly, I began to have that you're fucked feeling rolling around in my stomach. Oh, if I could only have called in an air strike right then.

Stunned by what this jerk had just uttered, I immediately spoke, but calmly said, "What do you mean, conduct? What you're saying makes no sense to me. It sounds made up."

Suddenly, it occurred to me, I wasn't here to receive help. I was there to be fired. I continued, but again, calmly. "Of course, I have no idea what you are talking about, and I'm sure neither would Steve. And for those of you who seem to be misinformed, I have in no way had an attitude toward my supervisor. As a matter of fact he hasn't even been around for over two weeks, he's been on vacation, and next week he will be in California on business, or vice versa, I'm not sure. So I think you have got your facts a little messed up, or made up, for that matter. If you people are confused or have me mixed up with somebody else, maybe you ought to get on the phone and have Steve clear it up for you."

After exchanging glances with the others in the room, the HR manager shifted in his seat and said, "Gary, I'd rather you didn't tell me how to do my job. If this weren't such a serious issue, do you think you would be here? What do you think this is, some kind of joke?"

I immediately replied curtly, "Do you see me laughing?" The fat fuck continued.

"The reason you are here is that we are concerned about your violent behavior and attitude problems, and that is all you need to know for now. So we agreed that you should be sent home as a threat to the workplace."

I quickly said, "It's obvious that you're making this shit up as you go along." The HR manager looked as if he wanted to try to hit me. Oh my God, do I wish he had tried that.

The HR guy shifted in his seat and said, "We're required to tell you that an investigation is under way, and there is a possibility you could be fired because of your behavior. But that is still to be determined." The HR manager pulled his lips together tightly over his teeth and slowly turned his attention back to my personnel file.

I looked at the HR manager and said, "Fired for what? What the hell are you talking about?" This asshole is lucky I didn't stuff Gus' Bible up his ass and throw him through the fucking window followed by Tweedle-dee and Tweedle-dum. If I didn't need the job to support my daughter, I would have had some fun that day, but I was trapped. They had me over a barrel, they knew it, and I knew it, and the ass-fucking was about to begin."

I looked up at Doctor Easton and said, "Never underestimate that little voice in the back of your head, especially when it's trying to tell you to fuck somebody up. When it tells you that you are about to be greased and ass raped by three self-serving idiot ass wipes, Gestapo's, believe the little voice."

Doctor Easton asked, "So, what did you do next?"

"After pulling a death stare from him, I said to the HR manager, "All right, you have to help me understand this. Please tell me what violent behavior you are talking about, because I have done nothing that even remotely resembles what you're describing because if you want my opinion, you're making it up. Are you sure you have the right guy?"

Michael spoke up for the first time when he so eloquently said, "Gary, he just told you what you're being accused of, weren't you listening?"

Yeah, I did, Michael, but I can also think for myself, and this is all bullshit and you know it. So this is the help you promised me?" Thinking quickly, it occurred to me on how they arrived at such a decision. Since they could not build a case on me by following me around at work, they must have read the VA paperwork I gave to Michael, and judged me by applying their own subjective view. Now, they find me a threat to the workplace. They're scared I might actually come in here one day and shoot the place up- what a bunch of chicken shit panty waists.

"I'll tell you, doc, none of those fuck-sticks were worth going to prison over. But I have to say, I understand when a guy goes into his place of work and starts shooting all the managers he can kill before he runs out of ammo. Now I know what the shooters are going through, mentally. And I totally support people killing the bad guys, Human Resources, I mean. I never regret seeing a bully die."

Doctor Easton said, "What did you say to them?"

I asked them, "Here's question for you, I come to you needing help and this is the way you assist me, by sending me home on some trumped up charge. I was promised assistance from the company in dealing with my PTSD, but I guess diversity doesn't swing the way of the veteran, now does it. I got to tell you, I'm a little disappointed in the way you people respond to veterans in need. I come to you for help, and you want me fired for some trumped up charge of being a threat to your workplace. If I'd been gay or an ethnic, we wouldn't be having this conversation right now, would we? If that were the case, I would've already been receiving help if I were a member of the LBGT organization, wouldn't I?"

The HR manager cut me a sharp look and said curtly, "How dare you judge us? I don't know what you are talking about. That other issue with your PTSD that you approached management about has absolutely nothing to do with what is going on here, or why we are sending you home."

That was bullshit and I knew it. I knew he was lying, I could tell. I was well trained from the military, and we don't miss shit like that. He was just trying to cover his own ass in case this ever came back on him.

I said, "You have got to be kidding me, you mean to tell me that you didn't have a gander at my VA paperwork and formed an opinion that I might be a threat to your workplace? What were you all thinking, because I am a vet, I might somehow come in here and shoot the place up? If that's your argument, you need to rethink your position because you've got it all wrong. It's not me you need to be worrying about. I got the killing out of my system when I served in the Marines. What you need to be worrying about are those employees who carry a grudge and have never killed, and you've got a lot of disgruntled ones here, bet you didn't know that. Those are the ones you need to be worrying about, not me. Those are the ones that will come in and make everyone meet Jesus."

I must have hit a nerve with that last statement. After hearing what I said, the three of them looked at each other, shifted in their seats and began looking around like someone farted. Fuck them. I liked seeing them squirm. I remained calm.

Then it occurred to me. This is what they were hoping for. They wanted me to lose my temper and get out of line. Losing my temper would be reason enough to fire me on the spot for insubordination. Something like that would be reason enough to cut me loose immediately. An investigation would only go forward if I never lost my temper and went home quietly like a good little corporate slave. I figured it out-they were baiting me, but again, I remained calm.

The HR manager then said, "Regardless of what you may think of us, we are here to help you, and in doing so, we feel it's best to send you home until we get this straightened out."

I cut in and said, "Yeah, I can see all the help you're trying to give me. Try not to do me any favors here will you, I don't think I could handle the excitement."

The HR ass-hat said, "I don't think I like your attitude. You better watch your mouth, mister. You need to understand we are here to help you. We are here to start an investigation into your current behavior toward your supervisor, which, as I said, has gotten out of hand. And let me tell you, this all has nothing to do with your PTSD."

I said, "Well, that's funny. It seems to me that the charge you are speaking of and my PTSD is one in the same. I've done nothing wrong here, and you know it's all fabricated. And whoever told you different needs to be brought in here so we can get to the bottom of this nonsense, because the three of you are starting to piss me off! And that's someplace you don't want me to be!"

"There is nothing to straighten out," my department manager said. "We are in compliance with the rules and regulations of the company in dealing with inappropriate conduct, and as of right now, you are being sent home pending an investigation, and nothing more needs to be said."

Hey, what could I do? They had me by the balls, and they had home field advantage. I was surprised at my manager, though. He never acted like this before he consulted the HR department. The truth is, they probably had a grip on his nuts as well.

The HR manager proudly handed me a confidential paper to sign, which stated that I was not to discuss anything that was said in this meeting, to anyone, and if I did, I would be fired. Also, I was to have no contact with anyone from the company while this investigation was under way, and if I did, I would be fired. And I was not to have any contact with Steve, and if I did, I would be fired. Fuck, why didn't they just go ahead and fire Steve and me.

I said, "I will sign your silly paper here, but I just want you to know, you're going to meet my lawyer. You're not going to like him, but you're going to meet him. The last guy he sued wound up killing himself. He's a great lawyer and he defends me jealously, so the two of you can start worrying now." The HR manager and Michael had darting glances at each other but said nothing.

After I scanned the bullshit piece of human resource paper, I signed it. Then the HR manager and my department manager signed it. My department manager then instructed the security manager to get my briefcase and escort me to my car. I waited in the room with the other two gentlemen when their other crony left the room.

Sitting there wondering if this were nothing more than a nightmare, I asked them, "Why are the two of you treating me this way, all I wanted was help? Is everyone around here afraid of me, or my disability, why didn't you just send me home with pay for thirty or more days? Or is something else going on here that I need to know about?"

Again with darting glances, the HR manager said, "As far as I'm concerned we have been treating you just fine, and when the investigation is completed, we will notify you of the outcome, until then you only need to know what we tell you." Didn't I tell you these people were the fucking Gestapo?

Then the HR manager looked away pretending to put his papers in order trying to look busy. I wasn't sure what was going on, but one thing was for sure, they had the upper hand by hanging my career over my head. I had to go along with their bullshit and try to solve the problem on my own.

With silence in the room, I kept thinking that if they could only read my mind right now, THEY WOULD FIRE ME. If I only had the power now that I once had in the Marine Corps, I would have the two of them violently killed and have it videotaped where I could have something to masturbate to later on.

Waiting patiently for one of them to comment about the weather or some bullshit like that, I had another comment, but the security manager returned to the room with my belongings. The moment he entered, Michael and the HR manager stood and didn't move, but they were carefully watching that I didn't spring from my chair to exact a little revenge. After what I just went through, I wasn't comfortable taking my eyes off them.

Once the security guard opened the door for me to exit, I stood, turned to Michael and the HR manager and said, "Stay close to your phones today, people, my attorney will want to talk to you, after he contacts corporate of course. Oh, and prepare yourself for a multitude of lawsuits on each of you, personally."

The security guard then said, "Let's go, son."

I turned and with all the intensity I could muster, I said, "You're only a couple years older than me, so don't call me son. And you smell like booze, you been drinking?" I then turned to the HR manager and said, "Here's your next victim."

The security manager stepped back and I walked out. I took my briefcase from him and then exited the east side of the building, stopping just outside the main doors. I had opened my briefcase and pulled out a cigarette and lit it when the guard said, "I'm afraid this is a no smoking section, you'll have to put that out." I lit my cigarette anyway and took a drag off of it before I stepped off the curb. I never put the cigarette out. I know that was juvenile, but right then, I was feeling a lot like the red headed stepchild, and whatever the guard had to say, meant very little to me, rules or no rules.

Walking toward my car I ignored his repeated attempts to extinguish my smoke. I got in, started my car, put it in gear and drove home."

By this time Doctor Easton was taking copious notes trying to keep up with my story. Doc Easton asked me, "What happened after you went home?"

Chapter Twenty-Four - Time Off

"Nothing really, I wasn't about to hang around the phone like some whore waiting for her John to call. There's a pub a few blocks from my house that several vet's frequent. I went there for hours, drinking and talking with other vet's about my troubles at work and how they are ass fucking me. If the company called, they could leave a message. Fuck them. They wanted me to go home and pace the floor wringing my hands praying to some fictitious god that I would not be fired. Bull shit. I drank a shit load of booze and brought home a good-looking gal from the pub and we drank some more. We ordered dinner, and the next morning we went to breakfast, all without me checking to see if the company called to hump my leg some more."

Doctor Easton asked, "I'm just curious, were you just threatening them with the lawyer, or did you really call one?"

"Oh, I did call my lawyer, the one from back home. Well, he really isn't my lawyer, but he's handling Mom's estate and keeping my brothers from suing me, and like you, I trust him. When I told him what was going on, he thought my story was interesting, from a financial perspective, I mean.

So he gave my company a call identifying himself as my lawyer and asking for proof of me being a threat to the workplace, and the names of the parties making the accusations. He told them he would wait for a call from their corporate lawyers and provided his phone number. He also told them he and his partners would be preparing a press release of how a corporate communications company takes aim at former combat veterans in distress, especially after he approached the company for help. Shit, I was impressed. We'll see. Maybe that will shake some HR monkey from their trees.

The next day I was saying goodbye to Monica when the HR manger called me. Once he verified it was me on the phone, he greeted me with his usual Gestapo fashion. "Gary, you are to report to work on Friday, tomorrow, in front of the main building no later than ten o'clock in the morning. There, you will be escorted to the designated conference room for your next meeting. If you are late, you will be fired. Do you have any questions?"

"Yeah, I have a question. Will Steve be there?"

The HR manager replied, "Do we have a problem here?"

"Okay, just to let you know, my lawyer will be attending this meeting with me tomorrow, and will be recording everything said, I'm assuming you have no problem with that?"

The stupid asshole said, "I will need to call you back."
I said, "Well, while you are checking, I will show up Friday with lawyer in hand." There was no response for the HR manager. He just hung up the phone.

An hour later I got a call back from the HR manager. Once he verified it was me on the phone he started to talk, but I cut him off. I said, "Just to let you know, I am recording this conversation per my lawyer's instructions. I was just supposed to let you know."

The HR manager then said, "There will be no need for lawyers at this meeting. We, the management staff, want to meet with you, it will not take long. Will you comply?

I was getting tired of this shit, and no job was worth being fucked and never getting kissed. I thought about telling him to shove the job up his ass and hanging up the phone. On the other hand, I was quite sure that's exactly what he wanted me to do. They wanted me to give up and quit. This way they would be off the hook for their fucked up behavior and wouldn't be held accountable. Fuck that-I couldn't let that happen. I had to fuck with them a little more.

The HR manager said, like the corporate robot, "Do as I say and show up on Friday or you will be released from the company for noncom…" I hung up the phone before he could finish.

Fuck showing any respect to that fat prick. You know who he reminds me of? He reminds me of the fat kid at school that no one likes, someone that's a tattletale, and is always getting his ass kicked and his fucking teeth knocked out just for how he looked. He's the kind of fat kid that will cry and run to his mother, just to have her fat ass show up the next day smelling like ass and feet, waving a finger in the principal's face.

What kind of shit was this? Released from the company for noncompliance, what a fuck head. Back in the Corps, their asses would have been tortured and murdered by now. But this was a different place and a different time, and the rules in the private sector don't run parallel to that of the Marines. I was powerless and I hated it. I can't stand it when someone has the power to pull my strings forcing me in the direction they want. If this was the military it would be different, but this was sloppy civilians, and definitely not worth my time, or going to prison over. Fuck them all. Let them burn, that's what I say."

With a concerned tone, Doctor Easton asked, "Gary, you okay? Do you want to take a break?"

Running my hands through my hair I answered, "Yeah, I'm a little worked up here. Can we take five?"

Doctor Easton said, Good, I'll get us some fresh coffee; you go have a smoke. I'll come get you when I'm ready to get started again. I walked outside where it was cold, but I could hardly tell due to how charged up I was from talking about my work issues. I sat on the bench just outside the main doors, leaned back, lit a cigarette, took a drag, and then something caught my attention. Looking up I heard a helicopter flying over and getting closer by the second.

(Our team low crawls into the jungle trying to avoid being seen by the enemy, it's dark, and I'm scared. For all we know the enemy is lurking just inside, waiting for an opportunity to pick us off one at a time. Maneuvering slowly into the jungle, all I could think of were the faces of the dead Americans killed in the ambush. The images of their lifeless bodies kept flashing in and out of my head, misdirecting my thoughts.

The moment we get into the jungle where we can actually stand, we hear several enemy soldiers running through the brush, and they're heading in our direction. Some of the enemy soldiers at the other end of the field must have broke into two teams, and are trying to flank our troops to have a shot at our incoming helicopter. The sergeant's right, the enemy wants that chopper, and we definitely have to stop them from knocking it out of the air. If they were successful, it would mean they got past the twelve of us, and we weren't about to let that happen.

Once inside the jungle, Corporal Crow, very quietly, set us up in ambush position as fast as possible. Each member of our team is armed and ready with excellent cover, which offers us the advantage for the first time in the fight. Looking to my right, I see the other members of our ambush team positioned in increments about ten feet apart, and waiting impatiently for the enemy to get within range. I'm so scared, because at this moment, ten things could go wrong with our plan, especially if the enemy gets past us. Not only will we be killed, the helicopter will be destroyed, and as for the rest of our team fighting in an open field, well, they will never get out alive. The odds are stacked against us, but we are confident.

Standing securely behind a tree, I hear the bad guys advancing, taking no caution as they move closer to our position. Suddenly, the soldiers stopped running, but continue to move toward us, walking, but with more stealth, and then, all is quiet. The enemy soldiers are some distance away but completely unaware we had slipped into the jungle and are waiting on them. The problem is, we can't see them, and they can't see us. All we have to rely on is the sounds they're making moving in our direction. As I listen for any movement, my guess is there are at least six to seven enemy troops, and they are well armed and ready for battle. I am nervous as hell, and I know that at any moment, Crow will give us the order to fire, to cut the enemy to pieces. And the scary part here is that I've never killed anyone before, and I'm not sure that I can.

Looking to my left, I can see into the open field and hear the helicopter approaching, but at a distance. Craning my neck around, I see Sergeant Yelims and the medical corpsman struggling to help a wounded Marine get out of the line of fire. The wounded man is out cold from the morphine, or the pain from being shot, and even though he doesn't weigh that much, the sergeant and the corpsman are struggling with every step getting him to the approaching helicopter. They're heading for our jeep in the field, which will be their only cover from incoming enemy fire. Unfortunately, there are four dead Navy officers inside the jeep.

Seeing the helicopter about to land, Marines in the open field toss smoke grenades as far forward as possible to provide a little cover for the approaching helicopter. As the helicopter touches down close to the jungle, three medical corpsmen jump out running toward the jeep, carrying what appear to be body bags. As two of them stop behind the jeep unrolling the bags, the other is quickly walking around both sides of the jeep taking several pictures before the scene was disturbed.

As the three of them work frantically to get the dead men out of the jeep and into the body bags, they know time is definitely an issue. As they work against the clock, enemy bullets ricochet off the side of the jeep, slowing their progress. Our Marines in the field worked hard protecting the helicopter as they continued to suppress most of the enemy fire from the jungle with heavy machinegun fire.

Once the wounded and the dead are on board the helicopter, the sergeant and our corpsman run back toward our troops, barely avoiding being hit by enemy fire. The other ten of our Marines in the field are securely behind several knolls, as they pop up and down tearing up the jungle in front of them with automatic gunfire and grenade launchers.

Just as the helicopter lifts up to depart, the enemy opens up with a heavy barrage of automatic gunfire from the tree line, but the helicopter isn't hit. Our Marines in the field immediately turned the M-60 machine gun, grenade launchers, and several more smoke grenades to give the helicopter a chance to clear the trees. The helicopter left unharmed.

Maybe Crow is right. Maybe the enemy did split into two teams. None of us knew how many enemy troops there are in the jungle planning to attack us. For all we knew there could be a hundred or more getting into position waiting for the right opportunity to overrun us.

What was worse, the enemy we heard moving toward us is now silent. We can no longer hear their footsteps or any activity for that matter. Either the enemy retreated back to their original position, or they know our exact location and are about to make their move. Jesus, we might have gone from the hunter to the hunted.

Waiting patiently, I squatted behind a tree. I was wringing wet with sweat and my hands were shaking so bad that it's a wonder I didn't pass out from exhaustion. Leaning forward to rest my head on the tree in front of me, I'm startled when we once again heard the soldiers approaching straight for us. But this time, they're closer than before.

Slowly, I lean back from the tree, raise my rifle horizontally, and then see corporal Crow with his hand in the air about to give the order to fire. The tension is high as I notice the other members of our team scanning the area, their fingers pulled tight across the trigger of their rifles. Our guys are ready to fire at any movement in front of them, and they are not about to take prisoners.

Suddenly, I heard an enemy's rifle bolt release, and when that happened, Corporal Crow yelled, "Fire.")

Before I had a chance to fire my rifle, someone placed their hand on my right shoulder. Startled, I quickly looked to my right. I couldn't believe it. I saw Dr. Easton leaning over me with his hand on my shoulder, talking, but I couldn't hear a thing he said. I was breathing hard from the fear of being killed, but suddenly, the sounds of the ambush were dissipating, and the sounds of Boulder were beginning to come into focus. I started blinking and Dr. Easton came in clearer, visually and verbally, and I started feeling nauseated. Dr. Easton then sat beside me with his hand still on my shoulder. He was looking at me with concern.

Once I looked somewhat lucid, Dr. Easton said clearly, "Another flashback?"

Nodding, I looked at him and replied, "Yeah, the second time today, doc."

"That's what I thought. Come on; let's get you inside. It's freezing out here, but you're warm to the touch."

"Give me a second, doc; I want to finish my cigarette." I pulled my cigarette up to take a hit, but it was already burned to the filter, which surprised the hell out of me, I had just lit it. I looked at Doctor Easton and said, "You're right, let's go in."

Chapter Twenty-Five - The Meeting

Once we were inside, Doctor Easton handed me a fresh cup of coffee and we both sat down in the conference room. I didn't say a word. I was just too embarrassed and too exhausted to get into what happened outside. Oh man, my head was hurting.

Doctor Easton said calmly, "Want to talk about it, or move on with your work issues?"

"If you don't mind, doc, I'd rather talk about my work shit right now, even though that makes my head hurt as well. We can discuss the flashback some other time. I'm ready when you are, doc."

Dr. Easton sat his cup on the table and picked up his legal pad. He looked up at me and said, "Okay, go ahead. What happened next? Did you show up for the meeting like they told you?"

Sitting back and running my hands through my hair, I tried to relax, but I had worked myself into frenzy, and my adrenaline was at an all time high. And with Doctor Easton scrutinizing my every move and comment, I was beginning to get a little edgy.

I answered calmly, "I did show up for the meeting. Upon arrival, I entered the building and was met by a security guard at the front desk. He smiled at me, and called me by name as he shook my hand. He then told me to follow him. Following the guard outside, he took me nearly around the entire building until we got to the southwest entrance. The guard scanned his card and we entered. A few feet into the building, we had arrived at our destination. We were in the most remote location possible in the company. We were totally out of the way of other employees and had a security guard by the door. The guard unlocked the door, opened it and stepped back for me to enter.

When I entered, the security guard introduced me to the HR manager, my department manager, and another manager in the company that I had never met. Once the introductions were complete and I took my seat, Michael, my department manager, wasted no time getting to the point. He informed me that I was not going to be fired, but would be written up because of my behavior, and that information would be put in my file. He told me that if for any reason my behavior became an issue in the future, I would be fired on the spot. These people were a mystery wrapped in a fucking turd.

Then, the HR manager handed me a company document, all official and shit, logo and everything, which I looked over carefully. I wanted to make sure that I wasn't signing over my inheritance from Ms. Birdie, or checking myself into an asylum. The paper indicated that I was being written up for unprofessional behavior, that I was never to drink on company premises, or bring weapons to the place of business, never threaten a manager again, or discuss the meeting with anyone in the company.

I wasn't sure if the document was written for me, because I had never drunk alcohol at work, threatened anyone at work, or brought a weapon on campus. Besides, if I did decide to bring a weapon to work, did they think I'd be worried about getting fired because of it?

There was one other item on the document that concerned me. It stated that I was not allowed to talk about the military or respond if asked about the military. For some reason, I don't think my first amendment rights apply in the company, especially if one was a veteran. If this shit ever made it to court, they wouldn't have enough evidence to fucking floss with, much less go to court with. After I looked the paper over I commented, "You know, I have never done any of what was on the paper, but for some reason you guys seem to have a hard time accepting my version of the truth."

The HR manager exchanged glances with the other manager when he looked at me and said in a condescending voice, "If you do not sign the paper, you will be fired. Do you understand?"

Hey, what could I do, blow away an eighty thousand dollar income over reluctance to sign a stupid piece of paper? They had me, and the fucking had begun, again. Fuck it, I signed the paper. But the thought of officially suing their happy asses still played in the back of my mind.

Once I signed, the HR manager put it into his briefcase and told me there was one more thing. He pointed his finger at me and said, "Under no circumstances are you ever to talk about what has transpired over the past few days, because if you do, you will be fired." I noticed that he sure got a kick out of using the word fired. Yeah, he had his ass kicked in school.

I calmly asked, "Just out of curiosity, isn't this a violation of my first amendment rights, assuming you have ever heard of the Constitution?"

The HR manager sat up looking as if I had just insulted his fat sister when he said, "If you want to stay employed with this company, you are never to tell anyone about what has taken place here today; is that understood?" That statement had me curious. They were on the hot seat here, and from their reactions, I'll bet anything they didn't have the authority to fire me, but just acted as if they did. My lawyer must have gotten through to them.

With a half smile on my face, I simply stared and never answered. I knew I was getting under his skin and that was good. Then they shared some more wonderful news for me.

The HR manager said, "I almost forgot, there's one more thing. You will not be going back to your old job. You have worn out your welcome over there. You are being moved to the shipping department. As a matter of fact, your desk has already been moved into that department while you were away. This gentleman here to your left is Mr. Cobb, he will be your new manager, and if you need anything, you need to see him, not any of us."

The HR manager stood, and everyone else did the same, indicating that he was an important man and needed respect. Fuck him, I remained seated. I have no respect to show him, or any other prick in the room. The HR manager said, "Gary, you may now go with Mr. Cobb, he will show you to your new office. I hope things go better for you over there." I remained seated and stared at them individually as they moved toward the door and out of the room.

Once the rest of them were out the door, I followed. Cobb, slob, knob, hand job, or whatever his fucking name was. I wasn't paying attention when they introduced him anyway. I followed him out of the door and down the hall toward the shipping department.

Cobb, my new manager was a fat piece of shit. Jesus, didn't any of these people know how to eat some fucking fruit or exercise, they were all fat asses. Slob Cobb stood about six feet tall, had a face with multiple pimples, and some kind of a rash all over his hands. He had more chins than a Chinese phone book, and a gut that ran past his belt well over his pubic area. He couldn't keep his pants up and was always adjusting and tugging on his belt or crotch area. I kept expecting him to grab his crotch and then smell his fingers."

Dr. Easton said, "Oh man, come on, you're making me sick." We had a good thirty-second laugh on my comments about slob knob after I pulled my fingers up to my nose and began sniffing. The laugh was good for me. It made my headache go away.

After our short laugh break, I continued, "Once we arrived in shipping he showed me to my desk. As I looked around the array of cubicles, I noticed several other people standing up from their desk to have a look at me. Well, I guess news does travel fast in a small company, as it was obvious somebody had been talking about the new guy's arrival that no one is supposed to be aware of. From the looks on their faces, it looked as if they knew more about what was going on with my situation than I did.

Looking at my desk, the entire area was a mess where the movers just dumped my equipment and personal objects. I began to slowly straighten up, but really didn't know where to begin. It appeared obvious to me that my stay in that department would be brief. The HR manager was probably already sitting in his office twisting his mustache preparing the paperwork. I hated these fuckers something fierce, but I tried not to show it. I was smarter than them, and my lawyer was better.

I had no idea how long it would take to get organized, or what my new boss expected of me. Cobb said, "Gary, I'm putting together a training program for you and another newcomer to the department. It will take me about a week or two to get it all organized, and until then, I'll give you odds and ends to do to fill your day. I heard you are pretty good at problem solving inventory and shipping issues, maybe you can work on that until the training program is under way."

"Yeah, that'll work. Just let me know." That was bullshit

on my part. I hated inventory problems. My training and experience was in negotiating and problem solving large corporate issues, not determining if we have enough cables to wire a communication center. You want that kind of information, call supply, not me, problem solved.

He said, "Well I'll leave you to it."

I looked up and said, "Yeah, thanks." Then he left and I was glad. I couldn't handle standing with him in my little cubicle with his body odor and his breath that was enough to gag a vulture on a shit house.

After a few days as the new shipping and inventory coordinator, and doing "busy" work, I noticed that when I was on the phone my line kept popping and had dead spots during my conversations. I knew Slob Nob was monitoring my calls and probably my e-mails, I just didn't know how much or how often, and I really didn't care. But anytime I got off a business call, I would stand up to stretch my back, and when I looked toward his desk, he was always on his feet craning his neck around to see if I was leaving the area. Of course, he was monitoring my every move. He should have followed me to the shitters. I would have let him listen if he wanted.

The next day, my new manager called me in his office to inform me that I was being assigned a workplace coach, and he would have my first meeting set up by the end of the day. He went on to explain how the company has a psychologist outside the company on retainer, and had set me up with an appointment. He told me the doctor's name was Rupert Gray. I just hissed and rolled my eyes knowing that meeting would ever occur.

So, I followed along and went to visit this workplace coach at his office where we could meet and discuss my so-called problems within the company. I arrived early but the door was locked. I waited for thirty minutes but no workplace coach showed up. After being there for over a half hour, I called the number Slob Cob gave me but it was disconnected. Man, was I in the fucking Twilight Zone or what? Fuck it, I left. I wasn't about to stay there all day. I returned to work, went to my desk and began working on an assigned task, which a fourth grader could accomplish. That was a week ago.

Then yesterday, Cobb walked into my office and asked if he could have a word with me. I stopped what I was doing and followed him from the shipping department into a conference room on the other side of the building where I had met him and the HR manager.

When he opened the door for me, well shit, guess who I saw sitting inside the room waiting for me with a file on the table in front of him? The HR manager was waiting for me with my company record sitting on the table, and with his usual look of distain on his face. I thought, here we go again. By this time, I was so dammed confused that I didn't know whether to wind my butt or scratch my watch. To be honest, I'd had about all I could take from either of these ass holes, and they could see I was frustrated. I was mentally shifting into Marine mode and that was not a good place for them to be dwelling.

From what I could see, Slob Knob and the HR manager had exhausted all avenues of trying to find things to fire me on. So now, I guess they thought bringing me back into the fold and making additional accusations about me might do the trick. I walked in and sat down with all the confidence of a negotiator, and not like a wimp that was afraid of losing his job. This trip, I meant business and I was not about to take prisoners.

After I sat down across from HR pussy, I asked, "Well, well, well, what am I in for this time, taking a company ink pen home, taking too long a lunch, no, no, let me guess, I didn't eat all my vegetables at lunch?"

The HR manager shot me a look of death when he said curtly, "You see, this is the type of behavior that got you sent home the first time."

I was quick to respond, "No, this has nothing to do with the reason I was sent home. You need to review your notes there, boss. You sent me home last time because you falsely accused me of threatening someone, which you had no proof of except for your fictitious accusations, remember. So who is it this time, am I giving Cobb here a rash?" Cobb then used one hand to cover his other.

"You are lucky I don't fire you right now Mister Sm…"

"Then do it. Personally, I couldn't give a shit what you do. I figure you brought me in here on another trumped up charge anyway, so why don't you save me the grief and fire me right now? I don't think you have the balls, and as you can see, I couldn't give a shit. I can't stand to listen to any more of your bullshit. So, if you have anything less than a promotion for me then you're wasting my time. So go ahead and do your business so I can be on my way to finding a real job in a real company with real people. I haven't lost anything in this fucking place, except sleep."

The HR Gestapo manager became very quiet and I could see him withdrawing physically. Actually, he looked a little scared at my response as he pushed his chair back from the table. Not that he was about to get up, but he pushed back in fear. I continued to stare directly at him. His right hand was shaking and there was a stutter to his voice as he tried to explain what I was doing there. Obviously, it wasn't to be fired.

Mr. Slob Cobb got up from his chair and stood by the door with his hand firmly on the handle ready to get the fuck out of there when I finally snapped. That chicken shit never expected me to rebel against authority, he thought I was just going to roll over and take it up the ass again. Now that he's about to run screaming to security like a schoolroom sissy, he would have second thoughts about fucking with me again.

In a shaky voice, The Gestapo prick said, "We brought you in here to inform you that we are dropping you a pay grade. Being in the shipping department does not entitle to the same pay grade as the negotiating team, so based on that, your salary will be reduced by ten thousand dollars a year."

Still fuming, I said, "Well, that's funny. I know of several people in the shipping department that are the same pay grade as me, and have been with the company less time than me. I don't see them in here anywhere. Why do you suppose that is?"

I wasn't surprised at their bullshit. Right now they wanted me out of the company so bad, they would have sucked a dick on the fifty-yard line, at halftime, at the Super Bowl, just to get rid of me.

Again I said, "I have been in my new department for, what, two weeks, and in that time you've evaluated my work enough to warrant dropping me ten thousand dollars a year? Is this your lame ass idea of getting me to walk out of the company, or was it Cobb's?" Still, there was no response to my attitude. I think they were too scared to push me any farther.

The HR manager said in a calm voice, "Your attitude has changed from our last meeting."

"Yeah, well it's a good thing you can't read my thoughts right now, huh?"

The HR manager said, "I just want you to know that as of today your job is hanging on by a thread and if you keep talking to us in that tone of voice, I will have to fire you.

"So fire me. But you're not about to do that, are you? As a matter of fact, you can't, can you? You don't have the power or the authority. You need permission because of the special circumstances surrounding my case and that comes from way above you. You all know that I came to you first, and now you have compromised the investigation by accusing me of some trumped up bullshit charge. When you came in here you thought this was going to be as easy as the last time you fucked me over, and I was just going to roll over and take it up the ass, well, you're wrong. Oh, just so you know, my Jewish lawyers are salivating over this case. They are waiting for you to fire me. They have a summons for all of you, suing you for millions. Oh, what a tangled web you weave, when you wear your job upon your sleeve.

"The shit stops here. If you want me out of the company then fire me and suffer the consequences. Otherwise, leave me the fuck alone, and you better not be fucking with my pay." Damn, Dr. Easton, I was on a roll."

Doctor Easton said, "Damn, I would have expected you to be fired after that exchange. Good God, what happened next?"

"You should have seen the look on their faces when I said, "Oh, yes, I know what you people are up to, and it won't be long before my lawyer will be petitioning your corporate lawyer, and your ass will be on the hot seat giving a deposition. And guess what, when I win my lawsuit and this company discovers you brought me up on some trumped up charge, how long do you think it will be before you are monitored and false charges are brought against you?" Looking at the HR manager I continued, "What did you figure you'd do after being fired, go to work for the government? That's a perfect fit for you there, bud, where you can operate with impunity."

Well, I guess I overplayed my hand a little. My intention was to stand up for myself just enough to get their attention, but once my mouth got to running, my brain had a hard time catching up. Hell, if someone had talked to me like that under similar circumstances, I would have fired their ass on the spot, and dealt with the consequences later. Unfortunately, I had gone a little too far with my attitude, they were genuinely afraid that I had gone over the deep end and might hack them the fuck up. I'll bet you anything they were told not to push me too hard for fear that I might snap and take matters into my own hands. I could be wrong, but I was willing to bet they had no intentions of firing me that day, just fucking with me so I would quit.

Standing up fast enough to make my chair fly backwards on its own, I walked over to the door, and Cobb backed away. I grabbed the door handle and said, "Fire me, don't fire me, it's up to you. You do what you have to do and I'll do what I have to do, and my lawyer will do what he has to do." I walked outside in the cold December winter for two cigarettes and then back to my desk to finish my work."

Chapter Twenty-Six - Walls are Closing In

"Sitting at my desk I was convinced that I was on the verge of a nervous breakdown. The walls were once again closing in on me, which made me appear to be looking through a fog. After about fifteen minutes, my phone rang, which startled the shit out of me. It was my workplace counselor, Doctor Rupert Gray, yes, the doctor I never met. He must have been calling from the back nine when he contacted me. He said he was calling me from his office outside the company, and began asking me how everything was going and if there was anything I needed.

Trying to think of a way to excuse myself, I just told him I was doing fine and coming along well, and had to go. Doctor Gray said, "Gary, I just received a call from the HR manager. He tells me that you were disrespectful, condescending, and arrogant. And they don't care what you have been going through, or who you think you know, they want you out of the company today."

"Well, doc, if you knew how I was doing, what the fuck did you ask for? By the way, I'm sure that you know our calls are monitored and recorded. There is no such thing as Doctor/Patient confidentially in this company, so be careful what you say, they may take you off retainer, or you'll wind up giving a deposition in front of a federal judge. Oh, and thanks for not meeting me at your office the other day, if that really was your office. I really enjoyed spending thirty minutes outside your office in the fucking cold."

"You need to listen to me, Gary. I don't care if we are being recorded or not. Right now your job is hanging by a thread, and they want you walked out of the company today."

"Fuck them, let them do it. My lawyer is salivating to get this case into a courtroom. You want to know what my lawyer said yesterday? This is the kind of case a lawyer can retire after. How about that shit? Dr. Gray, you want to be part of the solution, or part of the company that has to cough up millions of dollars because you chose the wrong side? When my lawyer sues someone, he sues everyone involved, which means you as well." After I said that, there was silence on the other end of the phone. I knew I was being monitored and I wanted the managers in the company to know about my lawyer's tenacity, and that Doctor Gray never met with me the day before, but he probably told them that he did. Busted!"

Then Doctor Gray said, "Okay, but one last thing and I'll let you go. I called your doctor at the Veterans Administration and he wants to have a meeting with you tomorrow morning at nine o'clock in Boulder. You need to be there. If you're not, there's nothing I can do to save your job. This is your last chance for survival in this company. Do you understand?"

Well doc that conversation with Gray was yesterday. I hung up on him, but you called me right after, so I must have hit a nerve with him or someone in the company. Well, unless you have some other questions, that's the end of my work saga. As far as I can tell, that is everything that has transpired over the past few months. If you have any questions, I'll be glad to answer them."

Dr. Easton said, "You really laid it on them heavy. I'm surprised you still have a job to go back to. I can't believe they kept you on after a meltdown like that. But you're right, maybe they couldn't fire you. Maybe there was a different agenda like you said. Maybe they were hoping you would just quit. I can tell now why you never trusted them."

"Doc, I never trust anyone, and I expect everyone to be a liar, that way I'm never disappointed in people."

"One last question before we move on to your military experiences. What ever happened to Steve? Did you ever get a chance to confront him?"

I answered calmly, "Oh yeah, I forgot about that. Once Steve got back from his vacation, I went to the bar he frequents every Friday afternoon. He was in a booth and had just ordered from a waitress. I walked up and sat across from him. He looked up and was surprised to see me, for sure. Steve looked around the bar, leaned toward me, and then whispered, "Hey, buddy, I don't think we are supposed to be talking. I have already been warned in more way than one by the HR director, that if I have any contact with you, I lose my job."

The waitress brought Steve his beer and asked me if I would like anything. I smiled, told her no, but thanks. Steve handed her a ten-dollar bill and told her to keep the change. She smiled, turned and left.

I said, "Steve, just to bring you up to speed here, since you have been away, the last three weeks have been quite interesting. The company brought me up on some bullshit charges saying that I threatened you, wrote me up, sent me home without pay, and made me switch departments. I told them there was no way I did such a thing, but of course that fucking HR prick already had a hard on for getting me fired and he's not about to back off."

Steve then sat forward and curiously said, "Wait a minute, I don't know anything about that. But something strange happened to me about three weeks ago when I was asked into Michael's office along with the HR manager. They both told me that I had too many vacation days on the books and needed to take at least two weeks off, and the sooner the better. But first they needed me in San Francisco to visit with an outsourcer for several days. What's strange here is that any number of guys in the department could have done that job, or I could have handled it by e-mail. Why I had to go there and then on vacation back-to-back was a mystery to me. And by the time I got to San Francisco, my trip there had been extended by four days, making it one full week I stayed there, doing nothing. It was a bogus trip because all I did was go out to lunch and dinners with mid-level managers, and attended meetings that I could have solved with a phone call.

Then I was told to book at least two weeks of vacation, three weeks if I wanted. Hey, all I did was what I was told. I got back yesterday and have heard people whispering and pointing fingers, you know the rumor mill. I heard from several people what transpired, but I never said a word to anyone."

Steve sat up straight, dimmed his eyes and said, "Gary, please, I can't afford to lose my job for meeting with you. You're going to have to leave before we are both unemployed-please." He put his hand out, we shook hands, I got up to leave when Steve said, "Hey, I wouldn't be trusting people in the company right now if you don't have to. Take care of yourself." I gave him a nod, put on my jacket and left the bar. As I walked away, I waved to Steve but did not turn around.

I shrugged my shoulders and ended with, "Well doc that was Friday of last week. And I hear from Aaron that no one has seen Steve around the company. Hell, who knows, they might have already fired him. Well, I guess that's about all I have to tell you about my job. I'll try to hold it together and let you and my lawyers work out the details in all this chaos."

Doctor Easton stopped writing, looked up and said, "Well, if need be, have your lawyer call me, I can give him any information he might need on your PTSD, as long as you don't mind him knowing what I know. If this ever gets to the courtroom, I'll be able to help, but I doubt it will get that far. And as far as your job is concerned, hopefully I can help you stay employed, but I can't make any promises, especially after your rant to HR yesterday, damn. Looks like you've got Human Resources pretty worked up right now. But I'll see what I can do."

"Do what you can for me, doc. I really need someone in my corner right now. Everyone else wants me crucified."

Nodding his head, Dr. Easton flipped to a new page on his legal pad and said, "All right, let's set your work issues aside. I think I've got a good understanding of what's been going on there, and then some. But right now, we're running out of time before the snow gets here, so I'd like to change gears again and take this opportunity to hear about some of your military service overseas.

I remember earlier you mentioned something about being an inspector for nuclear and chemical warfare. So to tell you the truth, I'm a little confused. The impression I got when we first met was that you somehow served in actual combat for over three years. And from some of the scuttlebutt I've heard from your medical doctor at the VA, you and your men saved some lives over there as well, and were decorated for your service. I haven't received your (SRB) service record book as of yet, but from where I sit, you appear to have a lot of combat experience under your belt. Am I right about that?"

I grimaced a little and said, "Well, I don't know what you heard from my doctor, but just to set the record straight here, I'm not a hero of any kind, not by a long shot. What I am is simply a Marine Corps weapons inspector that served as a rifleman- nothing more."

"So you were both then, NBC and a grunt?"

"Yeah, sort of, doc. I was a grunt but never attended an infantry school of any kind. It was never my military specialty. Hell, I didn't even know how to put on camouflage make-up, run combat maneuvers, read a map, shoot a machine-gun or call in an airstrike. And in most situations, I even had trouble keeping my helmet on. I might not have been a grunt or trained as one, but I became one, it's what I call being in the wrong place at the wrong time.

Don't get me wrong, I was trained as an agent of nuclear, biological & chemical warfare and I loved it. After nuclear weapons inspector training, I was sent to the Philippines, which was considered excellent duty for an NBC inspector. It was such good duty the Marines there called it 'Booty Station.' And, after being there for only a few days, I loved it. I loved the country, I loved the people, especially the beautiful women, and I never wanted to leave.

Unfortunately, my love didn't last. Before I had a chance to know what happened in all the chaos and confusion, I was thrust into an unimaginable world of death and destruction and well out of my depth for someone with no combat training. So just to be clear: Yes, I was officially an agent of NBC, but I also served in the field as a grunt for longer than I care to remember."

Doctor Easton said anxiously, "Yeah, that's something I definitely want to hear about, and we'll take that journey next week if you don't mind. But right now I'd like to get into some depth here about one of your military operations, the mission you considered your worst experience overseas.

Last week you mentioned something about a particular mission that took the wind out of your sails, but you never elaborated..."

With my thinking a little fuzzy, I interrupted, "Which one are you talking about, doc? I've been on several ops."

Dr. Easton sat up abruptly and continued, "Just give me a second here if you would. I think there's something in the shadows here you're not wanting to discuss, maybe even dodge." Dr. Easton dimmed his eyes as if he were in deep thought. He continued, "Over the last week I've wondered what it could be that would make you deflect in such a way, the most traumatic one, I mean, the one mission you would like to forget, the one that does not go away, my question here is: does it have anything to do with- a baby...possibly an infant?"

Doctor Easton surprised the shit out of me. I was taken back there for a moment. I knew this guy was smart, but damn, could he read minds as well? Somewhere along the line he picked up on the nightshade of my life that I've managed to keep buried for nearly forty years, but somehow, somewhere, Dr. Easton detected it. It's a secret I wouldn't tell anyone. Hell, I don't even like to be reminded of it, but I'm not that lucky. Unfortunately, my dark thoughts seem to creep through the cracks reminding me of a day long ago. It's a day I'll always remember, regardless of therapy I receive, the drugs I take or the alcohol I consume. I know I'm responsible for my thoughts, but what surfaces at various times, I have no control over, or how long it decides to stay... and that sucks.

It was obvious I was on the spot with Dr. Easton, because last week I did my best to dodge that particular story. Somehow I must have let something about the baby slip from my subconscious to my often uncontrollable conscious mouth, which often runs before my mind has a chance to catch up. What could I do? I was in the hot seat so to speak. So I decided to step up and finally tell my story. I took a deep breath, shuffled in my seat a bit, and said, "Yeah, okay, I remember the one you're talking about now, doc. If that's the one you want to start with, I'll tell it to you, sure."

Dr. Easton gave me a positive nod, leaned back, and began writing at the top of the page when he said, "Good, this one I want to hear! Start at the beginning."

I leaned forward in my chair and without any effort the memories began to flow as if it all happened yesterday.

Chapter Twenty-Seven - The Flashback

"On a snowy November morning in 1988, my wife decided to do a little shopping to find a gift for a friend. Due to the weather, I volunteered to stay home with our eight-month-old daughter and catch up on some reading. Besides, I needed some time alone, and I wasn't expecting any trouble from the baby. She would normally sleep through the day, and kept us awake at night.

Soon after my wife left, I fed, diapered and rocked my daughter to sleep and placed her gently in the crib. I tiptoed into the kitchen, poured myself a second cup of coffee and sat down to relax and read the morning paper. Then, after ten minutes of blissful peace and quiet, something happened that would forever change my life, and I haven't been the same since.

Suddenly, I heard my daughter crying from the other room. I quickly ran to her aid. She had just eaten and had her diaper changed, so I became concerned about the sudden burst of tears.   Worried that I may have done something wrong, I picked her up very carefully and began walking from room to room to comfort her. Regardless of my efforts, she continued to cry and kick her little feet despite my every attempt to calm her down. I then left my daughter's room and walked her around in the living room.

Panicking, and running out of options, I placed her across my chest with her head resting on my shoulder and began patting her back as I had seen my wife do a hundred times before. I wasn't sure why I put her on my shoulder; it seemed like the right thing to do at the time. Besides, it was the only option I had left. At first my idea didn't seem to work. Then, she burped, sighed and her little body relaxed and her eyes closed. Soon she was fast asleep.

Walking around my living room with my daughter on my shoulder, and feeling confident about my abilities as a father, I happened to look up and catch a glimpse of myself in the mirror. That split second somehow sparked a distant memory, which immediately set my mind adrift. That moment of confusion caused me to forget where I was, and mentally propelled me back into the jungle to a horrible day I experienced many years ago."

Chapter Twenty-Eight - The Village

"Well, doc, this was my second mission, which put the nine of us deep in the jungle looking for one specific man. His name was Jingles. That wasn't his real name, that's what he was called by the troops who ran jungle patrols. Whenever Jingles and his team were close or about to attack, the troops heard a bell ring several times. When anyone heard the jingle from the small bell, they knew an attack was imminent and they immediately went into Marine mode.

Jingles was our target, and for years he had eluded our jungle forces. As the sergeant once said, Jingles is responsible for every attack or death that takes place in or around the base, and we were looking for the opportunity to ring his bell.

Fortunately, our jungle unit received a report from intelligence that Jingles and a few of his minions were sighted some six miles from Dang Na Point. Based on the report, it appeared that something big was about to come down, and our unit needed to act fast. Without hesitation, Major Oaks sent our team out on a two-day mission searching a particular sector of the jungle for the most wanted man on the island.

Our mission was to simply observe and report, but in the event we spotted Jingles, we were to kill him on the spot. And we had the equipment to do it. The sergeant had a spotter scope, night vision gear and binoculars, and corporal Crow brought a .308 hunting rifle with a high-powered scope. We were ready. We were all well armed, and Crow, most of all, could not wait to place the cross hairs on Jingles' face.

An hour after receiving the news, we were on a chopper before the sun came up, and on our way to what was called a safe zone, which would allow us the opportunity to slip into the jungle undetected and maneuver to our final destination. We began just before dawn on a Thursday, and by nightfall on Saturday none of us would ever be the same again.

We had two days to locate the most heavily guarded enemy combatant responsible for terrorist attacks on our base, as well as the deaths of at least thirty Marines. We wanted that guy bad, and when we departed that morning, we were all convinced we'd be returning with Jingles' head on a silver platter.

Once we landed and made a dead run for the safety of the jungle, we cautiously scoured the area leaving no stone unturned, and we took every precaution to not be detected. During the day we searched our designated grid locations, spotting several villages and locals, but we never spotted Jingles.

At one point, we maneuvered to within twenty feet of three small villages and hid out for hours. We were so close several of the locals nearly brushed against us as they worked around the area. That's how close we were. As corporal Crow said, "All I need is one clear line of sight, and I will totally disrupt the enemy's high chain of command." Even though we were diligent and worked ourselves to near exhaustion, unfortunately, we came up empty handed.

After carefully stalking our prey, we found nothing but the hot jungle, the locals fishing in the river or tending to their crops. The next day, after a grueling nine hours in the sweltering jungle, we thought we had him.

While the nine of us were sitting in a small tight group whispering, the sergeant was about to call it a day when

Corporal O'Malley stuck his head up and said, "Quiet, did you guys hear that?" Immediately, each of us turned our heads trying to pick up on the sounds O'Malley tuned into. Sure enough, I heard it as well. From some distance away I could hear the faint sounds of someone screaming.

When we agreed that it was happening in a nearby village, the sergeant sent us into a defensive position. The nine of us then low crawled from our secure location through the jungle, closer and closer to the pleas for help.

Seconds later, Sergeant Yelims said, "You guys stay here and watch our back, Crow and I will move in closer for a better look."

Hyman said, "Oh, sergeant, this could be anything. Some old lady steps in buffalo shit and you guys want to check it out." Crow quickly cut Hyman a look, and Hyman kept quiet.

While the seven of us hid safely in the jungle, the sergeant and Crow moved ahead a few yards to have a better look at what was taking place in the village. Actually, I was eager to see what was happening, and I would soon get my chance.

As sergeant Yelims and Corporal Crow moved some thirty yards through the jungle toward the village, they stopped behind a dead tree horizontally in front of them. They peered over the log to see what was happening below when I saw them turn and look at each other with total astonishment. Sergeant Yelims then gave Crow a pat on the shoulder, and said something to him that I couldn't hear. They crawled back toward the seven of us.

Hyman said, "Jesus, I wonder what the fuck's going on out there?"

Doc scooted over to where Hyman and I were positioned and asked, "Hyman, what's going on?"

As Hyman craned his neck around a large elephant ear leaf, he quietly said, "I don't know, doc, but the Sarge looks pissed."

Seconds later, they reached us. Crow grabbed his gear and the sergeant whispered, "All right. Listen up; we're going to crawl back toward that log. When we get there, I don't want any talking." The sergeant then cut his eyes at Hyman.

The sergeant continued, "We have a major fucking problem here. I think the enemy's raided this village. We saw people down there being beaten, and some girls were forced into the shacks, where I'm assuming they're being raped. We'll watch the village for a while. If I'm right, Jingles might very well expose his ugly fucking head, and when he does, Crow's going to put an air vent right between his eyes. Come on; let's get back there. And we need to stay low and keep the noise to a minimum"

Quietly, we assembled and crawled to the outer edge of the jungle positioning ourselves behind a dead tree. From where we were positioned, we could see the villagers running around in a panic. I tried to get a fix on what was happening, as Sergeant Yelims opened his backpack and pulled out a picture of Jingles. While the rest of us were watching the carnage in the village below with binoculars, I saw that Crow was focused. He began adjusting the scope on his rifle, hoping for the opportunity to fire off at least one round. Corporal Crow was only looking for one specific target.

We were a few yards inside the jungle, but we had to be at least three hundred yards from the village. While looking through a pair of binoculars, the sergeant said to Corporal Crow, "Crow, if I spot him, I'll point him out to you. Don't shoot until you have a positive identification. Also, if you do shoot, we're going to have to leave here lickety-split to avoid being surrounded by a shit-load of enemy troops."

The sergeant then turned to Warfield, and whispered, "Move back a few yards, and call Division. Tell them what we have here and that we're about forty minutes from the extraction point." As the sergeant whispered his instructions, Warfield nodded that he understood. He then backed off a few yards and whispered into his radio handset.

Even with a clear view of the village, I had a hard time seeing what was going on because we were so far away, but from the sounds, I knew people were dying. While straining my eyes trying to get a good look, Hyman tapped me on the shoulder and then passed me the binoculars. I took them and zeroed in on the village with an excellent view.

Oh, my God. I had no idea what the enemy was capable of until I saw it for myself. The small village sat in an open area, which was surrounded by jungle, and was far away from anything to do with civilization. From what I could see, there were at least six huts sitting on stilts side by side next to the jungle, and not far from a creek that ran along side their camp.

It was a normal looking village. There were huts and they had handmade tools lying around, which were used for farming and cutting away vegetation. There were several fishing nets, spears, and woven baskets full of fish, which were drying under the sun. Not far from the huts, a dead pig hung in a tree but was left unattended. The reason was that the villager's daily activity came to a halt when the soldiers arrived and began tearing their village apart.

And there were plenty of bad guys to go around. From my field of view, I could see five of them hitting people with their rifles, and destroying anything the villagers considered of value.

According to the sergeant, the enemy sometimes raid local villages and take boys and men by force to have them join their cause. Sometimes the villagers do not resist and there is not a problem. But when the villagers resist, well, the enemy soldiers take what they want and then leave the village in peace or in ruins, depending.

At other times, when the locals resist the soldiers, like the ones we were observing, the bad guys get really ugly and do unspeakable things to show they are a force to be reckoned with.

With my binoculars focused, I saw three older men, probably the village elders, lying in a puddle of blood in the middle of the village. They'd been shot execution style in the back of the head with their hands tied behind their backs. Along the left side not far from the huts, I saw a line of palm trees, which had three elderly women tied to them. Whether they were dead we couldn't tell. But I could see that the women were slumped forward with their hands still tied to the tree behind them.

As I scanned the village I saw something that sent anger flaring through my body. I saw a woman, who could not have been more than twenty, running naked from one of the huts trying to cover her privates. When she ran out crying and screaming, I saw a man step from the hut with his pants around his ankles. He then raised his pistol, and shot her in the back. She fell to the ground and never moved again. The soldier pulled up his pants, lit a cigarette, and walked from the hut laughing and waving his hands wanting his friends to see him.

I said, "My, God. Did you guys see what happened?"

Hyman whispered in my ear, "To the right, look over to the right... Goddamn these mother-fuckers."

When I moved the binoculars to the right side of the village, I spotted what Hyman was talking about. I froze. Across the village, four of the enemy soldiers had several of the villagers on their knees and were striking them in the face and back of the head with the butt of their rifles. Two were knocked unconscious, or dead, and four of the villagers sat on the ground with their hands tied behind their backs.

Some of the younger kids were squat-sitting and not allowed to move. They were rocking back and forth, screaming as they watched as their parents being murdered in front of them. They pleaded and were reaching for their mothers to come to them. When one of the little girls got too close, one of the soldiers kicked her so hard; it lifted her up into the air. When she landed she was motionless.

With his high-powered scope focused, I heard Crow say, "Sergeant, so far I can see six dead, but there are soldiers to threatening to kill one of the babies. I can't make out what they're saying, but I think they're pretty serious. Oh, man, is that who I think...it is?"

At first I couldn't understand what Crow was talking about. Then, I saw it. As the villagers sat on the ground tied up, I saw that one of the bad guys had a baby girl tied upside down and hanging from a tree limb by one of its little feet. The baby was upside down and still alive, but she screamed uncontrollably and reached her little arms out for her mother.

But to my surprise, the soldier doing the threatening with the machete was not a man. The enemy soldier was instead, a woman. The female soldier, who appeared to be the one in charge, had dark black clothing with a black bandana tied around her head. She was yelling to her troops, and also threatening the baby.

She stood there screaming something at the villagers, and when they failed to answer to her satisfaction, she pulled her machete back and made a slashing motion toward the child, purposely missing it by only inches. When the female soldier pulled her machete back, I could hear the screams and pleas from the people on the ground rocking back and forth asking for her mercy. Oh, I wanted to kill that bitch so bad I could taste it.

When I leaned back to tell the sergeant I wanted to take her out, I noticed something was definitely wrong with Crow. The sergeant was talking to Crow, who had a look on his face like he had just received bad news. When I asked what was going on, O'Malley turned to me and said, "Smiley, you're not going to believe this shit. That bitch down there with the machete, guess who it is? It's Crow's girlfriend from town. You know, the girl he's been dating."

Surprised, I said, "What! You're kidding. That's Monica?" I looked through the binoculars, but I couldn't recognize the girl as Monica, but it was obvious Corporal Crow could tell. With his high-powered scope, he could count the fucking hairs on her hand if he wanted. So, there was no way he would be mistaken.

Then I heard the sergeant say, "Hurry up, take her out. I'm not about to let that bitch murder that baby. Do it, so we can get the fuck out of here before the rest of their cronies show up."

Crow was looking through the scope but he had not fired. The rest of us were not focused on the village, all eyes were on Crow. "Come on Crow, think about it. She's clearly the one in charge down there."

Crow pulled the rifle down and turned his back to the

village, staring off into the jungle in disbelief. The sergeant took the rifle from Crow and passed it over to me. It shocked the hell out of me. Did he expect me to kill Monica? I knew Monica. I didn't want to shoot her. I leaned the rifle across the tree, sighted it in...

I heard Crow say, "Hey, give me the rifle buddy." I took my finger off the trigger, pulled my eye away from the scope, and slowly turned to look at Corporal Crow.

Crow leaned over, took the rifle from me, and as I passed it to him I said, "You sure? I can do this, you know."

Crow looked at the sergeant, then at me, slowly nodding his head up and down in a way that indicated it was his responsibility. Crow then turned around, lay the rifle across the top of the log, and took aim. At the time, Monica was the only enemy soldier in clear view. The rest were destroying as much of the village as they could by setting the huts on fire.

The sergeant then said, "Listen up, guys. The moment Crow fires, we need to get the hell out of here, and fast, or we'll be dead meat in minutes." The sergeant then turned to our radioman. "Warfield, what's the status on that chopper?"

While talking into the handset, Warfield looked up and said, "It'll be at the extraction location in about forty to fifty minutes, sergeant. It's the best they can do."

As I watched through the binoculars, Crow fired. The shot was deafening as it echoed throughout the jungle. But with my binoculars focused, I watched as the back of Monica's fucking head came off. When her head came off, the rest of her body dropped to the ground like a side of beef, never to move again.

I then heard, "Let's go, let's go, move, and stay low people."

Five seconds had passed since Crow killed his girlfriend, and I was on my feet and in a dead run behind Hyman as the nine of us were running for our lives. Two steps later, I could hear the remaining bad guys in the village shooting randomly toward the jungle, not really sure where the sniper fire originated.

As we ran I heard Crow say, "Oh, fuck. Since we killed one of theirs, they'll probably take out the rest of the villagers now." After I heard that I knew everyone was thinking the same as me. Fuck it. Let's go back and kill the rest of the soldiers just to save the innocent people. But we didn't go back. Instead, we ran through the jungle in the opposite direction toward our extraction site.

As we ran, I could still hear the soldiers shooting. Due to the echo effect, the enemy had no idea of our exact location, so they just sprayed the jungle with automatic gunfire. But we were long gone and in no danger of being hit by any of their stray bullets. The nine of us were in a dead run through some of the most tangled vines and leaves I've ever seen. A couple times I tripped but was able to maintain my balance. Somehow, I managed to lose my helmet but at the time I couldn't have cared less. There was no way I was going back to retrieve it. That was the second helmet I'd lost in a month.

After a good ten minutes of jetting through the shit, and putting the village well behind us, the sergeant had us stop. Actually, we had to stop. There could still be several enemy patrols lurking around the area, and with all the noise we were making, we could have ran right up on them without knowing.

Oh, man, were we exhausted. As Crow, O'Malley and Valley took up a defensive position, Hyman and I kept a watchful eye as rear security, breathing hard and sweating bullets. Hyman struggled to say, "Okay, well, fuck this shit. I'm... getting out of the Marine Corps, getting my ass a nice comfortable job behind a desk, and I never want to see a gook or a rifle again for as long as I live."

Doc came over and with an out-of-breath whisper, the doc said, "Oh, man, did you see her fucking head come off. I had the sergeant's binoculars and I've never seen anything like it." While nodding and listening to the doc, I pulled off my pack and slung it over just one shoulder.

While gasping for air, I looked toward Crow and then back to the doc. I whispered, "Doc, try not...to talk too loud. I don't...want Crow...to hear you. He just...took out his girlfriend." While breathing hard, the doc, gasping for breath, looked at me and nodded genuinely.

As I tried to catch my breath, I glanced over to Corporal Crow, who had a beaten look on his face. But the look was not from the run or being exhausted. It was remorse, it had to be. Crow was pacing back and forth like a tiger in a cage. Crow was so full of hate and anger, you could have stabbed him in the arm with a knife and he wouldn't have felt it.

In the past when we're at the barracks, all Crow would talk about was Monica and how he wanted to marry her. They'd been together for months, and we were all surprised that he never popped the question. Actually, I had met Monica on several occasions, and not once did any of us think she worked for the other side. Crow loved her, and he had to kill her. He not only killed her, he killed her horribly. He blew the back of her fucking head off.

Crow had no idea Monica was, what the sergeant called, "A double agent." Crow met Monica at a bar in town and after a few months, he started supporting her and her family. Who knew that all along she was one of the leaders of a rebel movement, working in town around all the military personnel trying to gather information?

With a sixty-second break, the sergeant said, "O'Malley, Valley, get on point. Doc, you Crow, and Warfield stay in the middle. Smiles, I want you and Hyman to pull up the rear. Dixon, you and I will run flank. Let's go, and stay alert. We know there are at least ten of those fuckers on our ass looking for a little payback."

With an hour of daylight left, we still had thirty minutes of jungle to negotiate before we reached the extraction point. As we cautiously worked our way through the jungle, we could hardly stand we were so tired. We were exhausted as we struggled through the hot and humid jungle, tired, hungry, and drenched with sweat and stress. Not only were we exhausted; we still had the threat of being hunted down before reaching the safety of the helicopter.

On the other hand, the helicopter is not exactly the quietest of all the aircraft in the U.S. arsenal, and when one of them sweeps in to pick us up, you can bet your ass the enemy can hear it as well.

As we worked our way through the thicket, our radioman received word that our extraction chopper would be delayed due to mechanical problems and we should expect a forty-minute delay before its arrival. The only problem was, if we did encounter the enemy, our team would be stuck in the shit with no ride home. And worse yet, we would be wandering around in the dark with enemy soldiers on our ass, and they had home field advantage.

Since we didn't want to arrive in the clearing before the chopper, we slowed our pace but continued on as quietly as possible. Even though we were tired we stayed on the alert. Corporal Hyman slipped up next to me and quietly said, "Oh, man, after two days in this shit, when I get back, I'm going to fuck hookers till my balls drop off."

I looked at Hyman and said jokingly, "If you fuck a hooker, your balls might very well fall off." Hyman snickered and said, "Yeah, but what a way to die, buried in pussy."

Hyman usually makes me laugh my ass off, but when he was talking to me, I could barely make out what he was saying. I was just too tired, and too focused on the jungle around me and how quietly we were moving.

It had rained earlier in the day so we moved through the jungle without making a lot of noise. I heard nothing but our slow movement and a few small raindrops, which dripped from leaf to leaf. In a way the solitude of the jungle was quite comforting. Unfortunately that good feeling was about to dissipate. Someone either heard us or spotted us, or were cutting off our advance, but either way our lives were about to change.

Then, out of the dead calm, we began receiving automatic gunfire from our left flank. Whoever was shooting at us could not see us due to the thick of the jungle, and we could not see them. Regardless, we dropped to the ground and scrambled for cover.

Hyman, Warfield and I took cover behind some small trees and fired our M-14 rifles toward an area dense of jungle where we heard gunfire and the shuffle of jungle growth. Three of us sprayed the jungle from left to right and went through two magazine clips before Sergeant Yelims yelled, "Cease-fire!"

The sergeant gave us voiceless commands where we split into two teams and low crawled for a clearer field of fire on the soldiers. No matter where I moved, the jungle obscured my vision for any chance of getting a clear shot at our ambushers. Unless they moved or fired their weapons again, we couldn't get a fix on their exact location.

The enemy was firing and then changing locations where they would peel off moving away from us. They'd done what they came for and they were in the process of trying to leave alive, but we could not let that happen. If the enemies' intention was just to scare us, then why even fire on us?

Whoever our ambushers were, they had little experience at using weapons and I doubt they even knew we were Marines. For all we knew they could have been shooting at each other. From what we could tell, there appeared to be four or five of them some forty yards away, and even though they fired continuous automatic gunfire, they never came close to hitting any of us.

We'd been moving through the jungle so quietly the enemy couldn't get an exact fix on us. They were impatient, and since they didn't know our exact location, they decided to take a chance and shoot randomly.

The moment we heard the slightest movement, Sergeant Yelims gave the order to open fire. Whether they were experienced jungle fighters or just a bunch of local farmers, they still had rifles, and rifles kill Marines.

They again opened fire, which gave us somewhat of an idea of their location. We then laid down a relentless barrage of gunfire at our ambushers, and heard one of them take a bullet and yell for help. As we continued to tear up the jungle in front of us, the enemy soldiers stopped shooting only long enough to retrieve their wounded friend.

Suddenly, the bullets stopped for a moment, as the shooters began to retreat through the jungle in several different directions. The Sergeant then signaled for us to move out, but with caution. There was no way we could let the intruders get away. We wanted to know where Jingles was located and that meant interrogations were in order. If we let them get away, and they somehow managed to follow us to the extraction location, they not only could kill us, but they could possibly bring down the helicopter as well.

On the sergeant's orders, all nine of us got to our feet, and began to chase the enemy soldiers through the dense jungle. They were on the move and they were scared. As the soldiers ran from us, they fired off a few rounds behind them hoping to hit one or more of us in the process. While running in hot pursuit, we dodged trees, vines, and rocks, as we cut our way through the jungle trying to get at least one prisoner, wounded or not. But getting a clear shot became difficult with all the thick vegetation taking advantage of our inexperience negotiating it.

While we were running, Sergeant Yelims wanted to cut off their retreat, as he liked to say, "Head them off at the pass." As we pursued the soldiers, the sergeant signaled for me to flank the enemy from the right. Since I was the last man, I broke away from the team to cut off the shooters' retreat as the enemy made their way down a hill through a creek bed, and then up a hill moving to our right. Due to the jungle, we only caught a glimpse of them as they ran from us, and getting a clear shot was not about to happen.

While running as quick as the jungle would allow, I kept a careful lookout for enemy soldiers that might have had me in their sights. When I saw a clearing a hundred yards or so yards ahead of me to my right, it offered me easier access for a flank and a chance to gain ground on the ambushers. If I could get into that clearing, I knew that we would be able to take out one or more of the retreating soldiers. If nothing else we might be able to get a prisoner.

But to get into the clearing, I had to run up an embankment, down into a creek bed and then up the other side of the creek bank before reaching the clearing. As the other members of our team were moving farther to my left and exchanging gunfire, I came to a dead halt at the top of the creek bank. I stood there breathing hard and froze at what I saw beneath me in the creek. At first, I thought it was one of the shooters, until I had a second look.

Out of breath, I struggled to yell, "My God, corpsman... corpsman up. Doc, I need help over here!" As I scanned the vicinity for any soldiers, the other members of the team broke off the chase and swarmed to my location fearing that I had been hit. By the time they arrived surrounding me, and they too were stunned at what they saw. Sometime during the exchange of gunfire an innocent local was killed.

On the other side of the creek bed wedged between the roots of a Mangrove tree, laid a motionless young mother holding her infant daughter against her shoulder. Upon first inspection, we couldn't tell which one of them was wounded due to all the blood. Doc Sage quickly ran to their aid as the jungle fell silent around us.

The sergeant looked at me and asked, "What happened?"

"I don't know, exactly. When I ran up here to cross the creek to flank the enemy, I spotted these two in the creek, motionless. They haven't moved since I got here." I then turned to the doc and asked, "Doc, are they dead?"

As the doc stepped into the creek, the rest of us cautiously monitored the surrounding area, but for some reason I could not take my eye off the mother and child. I was no longer worried about the enemy.

While I stood there trying to catch my breath, I heard the doc say, "Hey, sergeant, the mother is not hit, but she's in shock." The doc then looked the baby over and said, "Oh, fuck. The baby took a bullet a couple inches below the right armpit exiting the left side." Doc then turned to the sergeant, and said in a somber voice, "Sarge, the baby's dead."

When the doc uttered those words, everyone turned to look at him. Shooting the enemy was one thing, but to hear that an innocent had been killed, well, that struck a nerve. All of our faces went slack like we had been given a shot of Novocain.

Sergeant Yelims shook his head, checked the ammo in his rifle, and calmly said, "Doc, take care of the kid. I'll speak to the mother. I want to know what the hell she's doing out here in the middle of the goddamn shit."

While the team stood guard, I watched as Doc Sage maneuvered around looking for the best way to approach the mother when she unexpectedly sat up all wild-eyed and tightened her grip on the baby, refusing to let go. The sergeant and our radioman, Warfield, waited patiently on either side while the doc once again made an attempt to pry the baby from her arms. In somewhat of a catatonic state, the mother refused to give in as she stared past the doc looking deep into nowhere.

I tried to remain focused on the jungle around me, but the mother and baby had my undivided attention. I watched as the mother sat against the tree staring off into the distance, and with her hands shaking, she began to pat the baby's back as if to offer comfort, but it was no use.

Then, in a low shaky voice she began to sing to her child in her native language as she tightened her grip. The baby only hung limp in her arms with blood and body parts soaking the mother's clothing. The baby was dead and the mother knew it, she just didn't want to believe it.

I looked over at Corporal Crow and Corporal Malley and they were just as upset as me. How could such a horrible thing happen, and the question was, who was responsible?

My heart felt heavy. I wanted to help her, I needed to help her, but what could I do. The damage was done. And the horrifying look on the mother's face, well, that's something I'll never forget.

We were all on guard expecting another attack from the enemy, but the jungle fell silent. After a couple minutes, Doc Sage managed to get the mother on her feet and the baby from her arms. The mother was light headed and used a tree behind her for support as she leaned against it and slowly slid back to the ground. From the expression on her face I wasn't sure if she would pass out or run screaming into the jungle. At that moment anything was possible.

When the doc passed between them, Sergeant Yelims and Malley focused their attention on the mother, wanting to gather information from her. Her baby might have been dead, but we still needed information about who attacked us, and the possibility of getting Jingles' location. If nothing else, the mother might have known the ambushers, where they were located, or how they were able to elude us, especially with a wounded man. We still couldn't figure out how they got away from us without leaving a trail.

When the doc walked away with the baby in hand, the sergeant and Malley began interrogating the mother in her language. Regardless of the barrage of questions, she just stared off in the distance as if she were someplace else.

With the baby in his arms, the doc cautiously climbed out of the creek bed looking around for some place to lay the child. I wanted to help, so I slung my rifle over my shoulder and pulled a poncho from my backpack. I shook it out and laid it flat on top of the creek bank to use as a makeshift body bag.

Carefully, and with respect, Doc Sage placed the infant onto the poncho and the two of us began to wrap the baby. We did the best we could, considering the circumstances. It was hard for either of us to look at the baby knowing what had happened to the little thing. I tried not to look upon the body but for some reason I needed to look.

Wanting to do the job right, I held the baby's arms together over its chest so the doc could properly fold the poncho tightly around the baby. When I touched the baby it sent a shiver up and down my spine. The baby was cold to the touch, limp, and her skin had begun to turn grey.

As the doc and I slowly folded the poncho, I glanced over at the mother noticing that she was ignoring the sergeant's questions. She continued to sit there motionless supported by the tree behind her, staring at the doc and me watching our every move.

The doc and I exchanged glances as we finished wrapping the baby in the poncho. When we were finished, Doc Sage leaned back on his boots, put his hands on his hips and shook his head from side to side when he said, "Fucking savages. How can anyone kill a baby?"

Looking at the doc I said, "When the enemy ran this way the mother might have startled the retreating enemy soldiers and they might have fired out of reflex. I don't know it's just a guess."

Doc Sage looked at me and quietly said, "Yeah, but a good guess, though."

Doc leaned forward, picked up the baby and handed it to me. He motioned with his head for me to give the child to the mother. He then turned to put away his medical equipment.

Carefully, I stepped into the creek bed with the dead child as the mother followed my every move. When I stepped through the shallow water, I handed the child to the mother. I couldn't help but notice the look on her face. Ignoring every question asked by Sergeant Yelims, she slowly leaned forward and reached out for the baby. She then looked up at me and stared deep into my eyes. The look on her face was that of death, hate, and revenge. I could tell she was looking for a little payback.

As the mother cradled the covered remains of her baby, she leaned back against a tree. As she looked at the poncho her eyes watered up and her lower jaw began to quiver. The mother placed her face over the poncho and her lips touched the poncho where the baby's head was. Then, all I could hear was that of a muffled cry.

Since the mother was not about to give up any pertinent information, the sergeant and Malley gave up on questioning her, and joined the doc on the creek bank. The rest of us then began closing in around the sergeant, awaiting his next order.

We still had the area secure, so the sergeant told all of us to step away and give the mother time to grieve over her loss. We cautiously assembled some twenty yards away and began gathering our gear and checking our weapons to prepare to depart the area. As we geared up, we kept a close eye on the mother, and the jungle. The mother was not a threat, nor was she any longer our main concern. We had to ensure the enemy was not about to flank us with reinforcements.

While standing only a few yards away and trying to maintain security, our radioman called to check the status of our extraction helicopter. He never mentioned to dispatch that we had come under fire, or that we had found a dead baby. That was a good thing. The reason was we still didn't know what to do about the situation. That is the first time any of us ever encountered such a problem and Sergeant Yelims thought it best to keep our mouths shut, that the baby was collateral damage.

As we all huddled in one area, the doc mentioned that if we leave the mother, she would eventually go back to her village, or wherever. On the other hand, the sergeant thought that if we took her with us, there might be an investigation into the child's death, which might jeopardize future missions for our unit and that sector of the jungle. It was just too risky to take her along, so we all agreed to leave the mother and to keep quiet about what had happened. What else could we do?

We then huddled in a circle when the doc suddenly said, "Oh, shit, where the hell did she go?" We immediately ran into the creek bed and searched the surrounding area, but we were unable to locate her. Somehow, she managed to disappear into the thickness of the jungle. After carefully searching the surrounding area, the mother and baby were nowhere to be found, and we heard no movement in the thicket around us. They simply disappeared. After searching the area, and not wanting to veer too far off course, we broke off the search and returned for our gear. We never saw her again. Well, that day, I mean.

As we prepared to move out, dispatch informed us that our chopper was in route to the extraction site, which meant we had less than fifteen minutes to get into the clearing. We had to hurry, and that suited me. That area was hot and full of activity and it was time for us to get the hell out before the bad guys left our bodies for the birds. Besides, it was nearly dark and none of us wanted to be out there at dark with enemy soldiers in the vicinity.

Sergeant Yelims said, "Let's get the fuck out of here before we get fucked. Fucking A."

With our gear in hand, we pulled our rifles to the ready and cautiously worked our way toward the pick up point to be airlifted out. Along the way, we saw no one, no enemy soldiers, or no young mother for that matter, just the sweltering jungle and annoying bugs that engulfed us.

You know, that was the time I was the most scared. We were moving rather quickly through known enemy territory with several bad guys on our trail, and we had no idea what lurked around the next tree or thicket. After twenty minutes of sheer panic, we reached the clearing.

When we heard the helicopter, the sergeant threw a red smoke grenade, which was verified by the incoming pilots. Moments later, two helicopters dropped in and hovered a few feet off the ground, and we were in a dead run as if we were being chased. As I ran, I noticed the helicopter about two feet off the ground and a crewmember hovering over an M-60 machine gun providing us with cover fire. I was glad to be getting out of there, and from what I could tell, so was everyone else.

Once we were safely in the air and out of danger, Hyman, Warfield, Malley and me huddled together and talked about the incident. We tried to understand why the mother was in the jungle right in the middle of a firefight. At first, we thought she might have been a lookout for the ambush team, but we quickly dismissed that reasoning.

Finally, we surmised that she was a local villager on an errand. We had noticed an empty bucket lying next to her; she was probably on her way to draw some fresh water from the creek when all hell broke loose. But that was just our opinion. What else could she have been there for, especially carrying a baby?

During the flight we all agreed we wouldn't discuss what happened with anyone, not even with each other. No one from our scouting team had a problem with that. It wasn't that we were worried about getting in trouble. That was just one of those situations where no one else needed to know. Personally, I had no problem with keeping silent. It's like what Sergeant Yelim said, "Who knows, it could have been one of our bullets that killed the kid."

After returning for debriefing, none of us reported a single thing to the lieutenant or Major Oaks about what happened in the jungle. We told him we spotted some soldiers but they were too far away and not worth risking the chase.

Once the lieutenant had our information as well as the grid locations of the enemy troops, he informed us that the Navy Seals would then put the ambush site under surveillance and mark that sector a hot zone for future operations. The major then indicated that our team would not be returning to that particular area.

That was good news because I wasn't interested in returning to that stretch of the woods anytime soon. There were some serious enemy personnel out there looking for a little pay-back, and no way was I looking to catch a bullet in the back from an angry mother.

Also, we stuck to our agreement and never mentioned the death of the child. I was surprised at how well our small team kept a secret. It was like President Harry Truman said, "The only way two people can keep a secret is if one of them is dead." Hey, I guess people can keep a secret when they really need to. We were all a little thrown off by seeing a baby killed in the line of fire, so it was easier than I thought to keep it to ourselves.

Furthermore, no civilians from that sector reported an accidental killing by Americans, which I thought might happen. They were locals, not enemy combatants. Not one question, concern, or suspicion ever surfaced as a result of the dead baby. It was like it never happened, and we were all fine with no one knowing. But that didn't keep us from thinking about and remembering that day.

With that nightmare safely behind us, our team all agreed that the best attitude was to write it off as an accident and that the enemy soldiers killed the baby. We had work to do and we decided to move on with other missions. Externally, we were able to keep our promise to one another and not say a word. But internally, it weighed heavy on our thoughts and our hearts.

Of all the Marines I've known, women and children tend to hold a special place in the hearts of Marines. Maybe that's a weakness, or maybe it's a gift, I'm not sure. I know it's what makes us Americans. We selflessly put women and children first, always protecting them, sometimes risking our lives in the process. Regardless, I try not to think about what happened that day. But it was like someone took a hot poker and burned the image of the baby deep in my mind. And for the rest of my life I would need to find a way to live with that mental scar at the beginning of all my thoughts.

A few days after we returned, the other members of the team eventually put what happened behind them, and their attitudes and emotions slowly returned to normal. Wolf said that trying not to remember what happened was like moving around in slow motion while you're on fire. During our off time, we were hitting the bars and the team seemed to be getting back to their old selves again, and the alcohol didn't hurt. Even though the team began to adjust, I played along as if nothing were troubling me. I definitely was not the same and I knew the others were not either.

On a daily basis my gut felt like it was churning glass. Besides the depression, I also had a difficult time sleeping and staying focused. In my mind all I could see was the cold dead body of an infant and a grieving mother who was suffering far more than anything we could feel guilty about.

Then, as the days and weeks passed and new challenges arose, I was eventually able to set those thoughts aside. I, too, moved on with my life until that horrible day resurfaced to remind me of the mental scar I now carried.

Even though it had been many years since my encounter with the mother and her baby, that vivid memory resurfaced with such clarity, that it became difficult for me to distinguish between the past and present.

But on that day back in 1988, with my own child lying on my shoulder and then catching a glimpse of myself in the mirror, it took my mind into uncharted territory.

With my thoughts drifting in and out, I managed to catch myself sitting on the living room floor with my daughter, where I had begun to tightly wrap her entire body in her green baby blanket. By the time I realized what the hell I was doing my daughter was struggling to get free, about to suffocate. Once I realized where I was, and what I was doing, I pushed myself backwards away from my baby to collect my thoughts. Then, while I was still lucid, I quickly removed the blanket and placed my daughter back in her crib, where she cried herself to sleep.

I was so upset at myself for having such a flashback that my hands shook uncontrollably, and I was hyperventilating. It was then time for a drink. From that moment on I monitored my daughter from a distance. My daughter was fine, but I wasn't.

After my wife returned from shopping, I never mentioned the incident with the baby blanket or the flashback. Some things are best left unsaid, and I was really good at holding on to secrets. After that day, I didn't even approach her crib for several days, and I never stayed home alone again with my daughter until she was walking and talking.

It seemed my problems dealing with past memories somehow manifested into my first flashback, or whatever it's called. Regardless, it scared the living shit out of me. After seeing where my mind had taken me, and the thought of nearly killing my daughter, I thought about seeking help from the Veteran's Administration as a way to get my thoughts under control and to regain control of my life. It was a great idea but I never sought help until I met with you a week ago.

Following my tour in the Marines, and all the shit I had been through, the incident with the mother and baby were the most traumatic. It totally fucked up my soul and every nerve associated with it. I can't help to think that somewhere overseas an innocent child was killed in some bullshit half-ass military operation that was not necessary, didn't have to happen and will never be remembered, except by the ones involved. Regardless, the baby is still dead, but did her death do anything to stop firefights in the jungle? Or did her death solve all the problems in that part of the world, or was she just collateral damage where countries are so immature that we have decided that we have to kill each other, including children in order to make us all feel more like grown-ups. I keep thinking where the baby would be today if our paths had not crossed that day. Today, that baby would be over forty years old, and a mother herself. But now she no longer exists, except in my memory."

I paused for a moment to sip my coffee. Looking at Doctor Easton, I could tell he was focused on the end of my story. He remained quiet, taking in this new information, analyzing me with his eyes, absorbing every word, and my lack of emotions. I couldn't tell what he was thinking, but the room was silent with just the two of us sitting and looking at each other. It was so quiet you could hear a fish fart.

In a curious voice, Doctor Easton asks, "How do you feel right now, buddy?"

"I'm okay. I felt it was time to come clean, so clean that I feel dirty again. I've held on to that piece of history for way too long, and because of that, it's created an empty void deep inside that no alcohol, pain pills or anti-depressants can tame. I not only lied to everyone around me, I deceived myself thinking that I somehow had control. You know what they say in the Marines, "Oh, what a tangled web we weave, when we first fail to grieve."

In a low sincere voice, Doctor Easton said, "That's good information; I know that must have been hard to talk about. I appreciate you sharing."

I looked at Doctor Easton and said with a smile, "Well, that's my story, but it's not the whole story, or the end of the story, which still needs to be told. That's for sure."

Dr. Easton stopped writing, smiled, pointed at me and said, "To be continued. How about five days from now, on the 28th, three days after Christmas?"

"Done."

Chapter Twenty-Nine - The End of the Journey

In a quiet voice Dr. Easton asked, "Well, that's all the questions I have to ask at this time, and that's all the answers you'll need to give right now-thank god, right?" He then smiled at me and stood up. "I will pass on this new information and my recommendations to our psychiatrist, Doctor Young. We'll have a chat and we should have a decision for you in a day or two. But don't worry; things have a way of working out. Remember, you've got me in your corner!"

Dr. Easton and I walked to my jeep making small talk as he mentioned that it was supposed to snow and it was cold as hell outside. The questions might have been over but I could tell he still had something on his mind.

I opened the door to my vehicle, stepped in, and rolled down the window when Dr. Easton asked with a curious tone, "So, off the record here. Which one of you killed the baby?"

I buckled myself in the jeep, started the engine, and then said with a smile, "To be continued!"

Dr. Easton smiled, began nodding his head knowing that there would be no more answers coming from me today. Using his hand, Dr. Easton gave the hood of my jeep a couple taps then he backed up. I put out my hand to wave goodbye when he yelled out with a smile, "Damn straight to be continued. Remember the 28th, we'll talk, I want your entire story next time!" Doctor Easton turned and quickly stepped back into the building rubbing his hands together.

I smiled and drove onto the street and two blocks later I pulled into another parking lot of a local coffee shop. All I wanted was a good cup of coffee to keep me warm on my long drive home. I stopped the jeep, turned off the engine, and as I reached for the door handle. I caught a glimpse of something off to my right. There, walking into the coffee shop was a young Asian mother with her baby all bundled up in a green blanket. When she caught me looking at her, she gave me a double take, smiled, and then hurried to the entrance to get out of the cold. Sitting there for a few seconds, I started the engine, pulled out of the parking lot, and said out loud to myself, "Well, fuck me, guess who's not going to sleep tonight!!"

The End